Before The Flower Wi...

Dedication:

To my sister Vicky, a beautiful rose in my life who fought valiantly against many cancers and beat them. She sang and danced, and did things her doctors told her she couldn't do. One doctor called her 'one tough cookie!' Her motto was: Live, Laugh, and Love always! To my dearly departed Mother Maria (Mana). And to my Godmother (Newna) Cleo, and my Mother-In-Law Jeanette, the other 'Moms' and beautiful flowers in my life who are also real tough cookies! These and others in my life like them inspired me to create and write this story.

Prologue:

Rose Miles is a 75 year old woman suffering from terminal cancer. When her compassionate grandson Russ Barnett learns she has less than six months to live, he dedicates his time to help her create and carry out a bucket list. Every time they venture out to accomplish goals from her list, they encounter a combination of heartwarming and comical situations. Join Rose as she faces her final days with laughter and excitement. You'll be moved by her amazing courage and strength.

Before The Flower Withers   by Dennis C Mariotis

Before The Flower Withers

by Dennis C Mariotis

U.S. Copyright Registration # TX 8-789-045

September 6, 2019

All rights reserved. No part of this publication may be reproduced, distributed, or transmitted in any form or by any means without the prior written permission of the author, except in the case of brief quotations embodied in critical reviews and certain other noncommercial uses permitted by copyright law.

Disclaimer: This book is a work of fiction. Names, characters, businesses, places, events and incidents are either the products of the author's imagination or used in a fictitious manner. Any resemblance to actual persons, living or dead, or actual events is purely coincidental.

Front Cover Photo was taken by Dennis C Mariotis

Back Cover Photo was taken by Anastasia C Mariotis.

Before The Flower Withers   by Dennis C Mariotis

A special note from the Author:

This book is not as long as I originally intended to write it. I omitted many details regarding defining the physical attributes of the main characters, Rose and Russ, as well as the others. This was intentionally done with a specific purpose. That purpose is to let the reader's imagination picture the characters rather than the author's portrayal of each character. The reason I did this is because most, if not all who read this book, know of or have been personally impacted by someone like (male or female) Rose or Russ in their lives. The reader may even have been in, or is currently experiencing, the same situation as any of the characters just as I did in my life. I want the reader to have a personal experience by picturing that person or persons from their life throughout the story. If you do this, then I succeeded in my purpose. If not, I believe you will still thoroughly enjoy reading this book as you follow Rose's adventures as she enjoys the final chapter of her life.

Thank you!
Live, Laugh, and Love always,
    Dennis C Mariotis

Before The Flower Withers   by Dennis C Mariotis

CHAPTER 1
Rose and Russ

"You look worried doc!" exclaimed Rose. "Well Rose, after reviewing the results from the additional imaging scans I consulted with two other Oncologists separately and they confirmed exactly what I saw," replied Dr. Bill as he put Rose Miles's medical file down, sighed, removed his eyeglasses and rubbed his eyes. He paused as he stared at Rose for a few

Before The Flower Withers   by Dennis C Mariotis

seconds. Reading his concerned expression and realizing the doctor was thinking of how he was going to tell her the bad news, Rose didn't wait for him. With a stern look and a serious tone, she demanded, "I'm a big girl! Give it to me straight Bill!...*How bad is it?*"

Leaning forward he shook his head and answered, "It's very bad. The treatments you underwent didn't stop the cancer and it's spreading throughout your body." Rose sighed as she looked up at the ceiling. Returning her focus on the doctor she asked, "Are there any other treatments that can help or should I go home and select the last outfit I'm gonna wear?" Shaking his head the doctor answered, "We tried almost every treatment available. The only other choice we have left is a stem cell transplant." Rose asked, "What's involved with that?" Dr. Bill explained, "It's an extensive series of very rough and painful procedures using chemotherapy and radiation and you're going to be in an isolation room for a while depending on how you respond." In

Before The Flower Withers   by Dennis C Mariotis

a frustrated tone Rose asked, *"What are my chances with that?!"* The doctor shook his head answering, "Not very good. About a three percent chance, **IF** you survive the treatment! If you choose not to do this then I believe you'll only have anywhere from four to six months."

Staring at the doctor in disbelief she shook her head and in an irritated tone she responded, *"IF, I survive the treatment?.... Bill, I'm seventy-five years old...and I've all ready been through a great deal of pain and anxiety with all the treatments up till today. What you're telling me is that modern medical science can't do anything more...and it's basically over for me!"* Dr. Bill clenched his teeth, nodded, and apologetically replied, "I'm sorry Rose. There are no other treatments that'll help you."

Rose pursed her lips and looked down at the floor. Then she rubbed her forehead and thought for a moment. Lifting her head and looking up at Dr. Bill she cleared her throat and

Before The Flower Withers   by Dennis C Mariotis

said, "So my choice is either go home and live however long I have until I die...or take my chance with a procedure that **will** put me through more anxiety and torture with little to no chance of survival." Nodding after a few more seconds she said, "I've had enough chemotherapy and been burned with all those radiation treatments, and I don't want anymore. I'm going with option A. I'm gonna go home and be around my family for whatever time I have left!"

        Dr. Bill nodded in agreement and with empathy he replied, "I totally understand. I've been your physician for a long time and you're a remarkably strong and sensible woman. Given what you have, if it was me, I would probably do the same thing. I'll prescribe some pain medication for you. Call me if you have any questions or if you want to talk to me about anything. I'm sorry I can't do anything more for you." Rose asked, "One more question Bill: How will I know when the end is near?"

Before The Flower Withers   by Dennis C Mariotis

The doctor looked Rose in the eyes and answered, "Everyone experiences different symptoms. The most common are; constant weakness and loss of breath after minor effort, difficulty breathing while you're resting, extreme fatigue, forgetfulness, anxiousness, a boost of energy from seemingly out of nowhere, restlessness, severe pain that you've never had before, your hands and legs may get cold and numb, and skin discoloration. Your imagination can have you seeing people who died before you. Many times there's a feeling of peacefulness. When the time gets close, you'll know it."

Rose shook her head, looked up and sighed, then looked at Dr. Bill and chuckled when she replied, "If I ignore these symptoms will it go away?" Dr. Bill smiled, "I'm afraid not, but I strongly suggest that you make the most of whatever time you have left. You're one tough cookie Rose, and if anyone can fight the Grim Reaper, my money's on you!" She maintained her composure and said, "I plan to go the

Before The Flower Withers   by Dennis C Mariotis

distance! Thanks for doing your best Bill." They stood up. Dr. Bill walked around his desk to Rose and gave her a hug. The doctor nodded as he watched Rose turn and walk out of his office.

Standing outside the doctor's office and hearing the entire conversation was Rose's twenty-four year old grandson Russ Barnett. Upon hearing the conversation ending, Russ raced back to the waiting room, sat down, and crossed his legs. He quickly picked up a magazine, opened it to a random page, and pretended as if he was engrossed in it. He sat in the chair and kept his composure as Rose exited the doctor's office, and walked into the waiting room.

Walking up to him, she stopped and said, "Well I'm ready to go. C'mon Russ." With a half hearted attempt at a smile, Russ looked up at her and said, "Ok grandma," as he put down the magazine, stood up, and offered his arm to her. She smiled and winked at him as she hooked his arm and together they walked out of the office

***Before The Flower Withers**   by Dennis C Mariotis*

building to his car in the parking lot. Russ opened the door and waited for her to sit down comfortably before closing it. He then walked around to the driver's side, entered the car, and drove off.

"How'd your follow up go?" asked Russ with a little nervousness in his voice. Rose looked at Russ and answered, "Just fine. Dr. Bill told me I'm one tough cookie." Continuing to question her he asked, "How about the results from all your tests?" Rose studied his expression, then snickering she answered, "Oh you know... Eat more greens, exercise, get plenty of fresh air...and maybe I'll live another year." Russ glanced at Rose and returned the laugh. He noticed her growing suspicions from his questions, so the rest of the way home it was small talk between them, and nothing related to her health and doctor visit.

Parking in the driveway of her home, Russ exited his car and walked to the passenger side where he

Before The Flower Withers   by Dennis C Mariotis

opened the door to help her out. "Thanks for helping me today Russ. You've always been there for me." said Rose as she hugged him and kissed his cheek. "You're welcome grandma. Call me anytime you need me and I'll be there." Seeing his serious expression she asked, "I made my world famous cheesecake. How about coming in for a slice and a glass of milk?" He smiled and said, "Sure. You know how much I love your cheesecake." Closing the passenger door and locking his car, Russ and Rose walked up the front steps to her house. She unlocked the door and entered as Russ followed behind her. There to greet them was Rose's fat pet cat Tuffy, who waited for them to enter the house before meandering back to his soft cushy bed in the corner.

After putting away her purse and paperwork from the doctor's office, Rose walked into the kitchen. Russ was sitting at the table waiting for her. She opened the refrigerator and pulled out the cheesecake along with a quart of milk. Setting them on the table she put a plate and glass in

Before The Flower Withers   by Dennis C Mariotis

front of him, then she cut a piece of cake as Russ poured himself a glass of milk. After savoring a large bite of cheesecake along with a big gulp of milk, Russ smiled at Rose, and said, "This is heaven!" With another half hearted smile and a little nervousness in his voice, he looked down at the cake and continued, "Nobody makes this like you grandma." Swallowing hard he looked back at her and forced another smile.

Realizing and understanding the sad expression behind his smile she reached over and patted his hand. Containing his emotions Russ had an idea. Working on keeping his composure and a straight face he said, "Grandma. I was doing some thinking and I decided I'm gonna take this summer off so I could spend some time with you, my mom, and my brother. What do you think about that?" Rose became more suspicious. She asked, "But you're doing so well and you're on a roll. What made you decide to take a break?" Catching him off guard he looked away for a few seconds, then answered, "I

Before The Flower Withers   by Dennis C Mariotis

just wanna spend some quality time with everyone in my family before I go on to grad school."

Rose studied him, and seeing right through his body language she asked, "I can tell something's bothering you. What's wrong Russ?" Trying to fake it, Russ knew she caught on as he leaned back and answered, "Nothing. Why do you ask?" She snickered answering, "Oh c'mon honey. I changed your diapers. Don't you think I know when you're full o' crap?" Russ shook his head as they laughed.

With a serious look she said, "You can't fool this ol' bird. You know about the cancer, don't you?" Russ fought off his emotions as he stared down at his cheesecake. He swallowed hard again and nodded. In a serious concerned soft tone he looked at Rose, then he closed his eyes and answered, "Yeah." Rose inquired, "How did you know?" Russ looked up at the ceiling and sighed, then turned his attention back to Rose, "Dr. Bill looked very serious and upset when he

***Before The Flower Withers**   by Dennis C Mariotis*

walked into his office with you. I walked up to the door and eaves-dropped on the conversation." Russ stood up, stepped over to Rose and hugged her. With a bit of cracking in his voice he sadly said, "I'm so sorry grandma!"

      Being strong for Russ' sake, Rose chuckled through her sadness as she hugged him, "That's OK. You saved me the trouble of figuring out how I was gonna break the news to you. Do me a favor and don't tell your mom or anyone else. Let me do that later tonight." Russ kissed her cheek, and then nodded as he broke his embrace. He walked back and sat in his chair, and with sadness, he stared down at his plate. She looked at him and smiling she said, "Don't worry Russ. I'm not gonna leave this world without a fight!" Russ looked at Rose, smiled and said, "My money's on you too grandma!"

Before The Flower Withers   by Dennis C Mariotis

CHAPTER 2
Rose's Life

A few days later on a beautiful Saturday morning in Marietta, Georgia it was time for Rose's yard to be mowed. Russ arrived at nine a.m. sharp. He went to the shed where he filled the lawn mower with gas and checked the oil. He exited the shed and parked the mower by the back door which led to Rose's kitchen. Walking up to the door he was about ready to knock when he heard Rose talking loudly. Listening closely with his ear pressed

Before The Flower Withers   by Dennis C Mariotis

against the window part of the door he realized Rose was having a loud angry conversation with herself. When the conversation stopped he leaned his body against the door and pressed his ear harder against the glass.

Suddenly the door quickly opened and surprised Russ as he lost his balance. Falling onto the kitchen floor momentarily disoriented him. Regaining his composure he sat up and looked up at Rose who stood in front of him holding onto the doorknob of the opened door. Smiling at him Rose chuckled and said, "Eaves-dropping again? This is getting to be a terrible habit with you!"

With an embarrassed smile Russ stood up and approached Rose. Giving her a hug he replied, "Sorry grandma but I heard you shouting and you sounded really angry. I didn't know if there was anyone here causing you some trouble and I just wanted to be sure you were all right. Then I realized you were talking to yourself."

Before The Flower Withers   by Dennis C Mariotis

Rose chuckled, "Since your grandpa died a couple of years ago I've been alone, and I have no one else to talk to so I talk to myself. It's very therapeutic by letting out stuff in my head and not keeping it bottled up inside!" Snickering, she jokingly continued, "Besides, I like the conversation and the company. And it's always a very intelligent conversation." Russ laughed at her explanation and asked, "But why the loud angry tone?" Rose's smile turned to a serious expression when she answered, "Because I thought about what a short time I have left in this world! I was having a bad moment and I was mad at everything. I scared Tuffy so bad, he ran off and hid under the bed." Russ gave her a sympathetic stare and said, "I completely understand." Rose stared back, then she shook her head and replied, "Actually Russ, you can't possibly understand what I'm feeling." Russ was puzzled and squinted his eyes as he tried to comprehend her reply. He asked, "Well tell me what it is you're feeling grandma?" Rose took a deep

Before The Flower Withers   by Dennis C Mariotis

breath, then let out a long sigh and with a frustrated expression she replied, "I feel like I haven't done anything worthwhile and fun with my life and now there's no time left to do anything!"

Russ felt sorry for her and hugged her again. Letting go and stepping back he looked her in the eyes and asked, "What do you mean? Of course you've done a lot of things. You grew up in a great family. You married a fine man in grandpa. You raised a family of your own, and you were healthy enough to live long enough to see your grandkids grow up. That's more than a lot of other people have done."

Rose looked at Russ and nodded, then she replied, "I know. And you're right to some degree, and I'm very blessed, and glad for all those things. But taking care of a home, your grandpa, and raising a family took **all** of my time. When your mom and her sister got married and moved out, grandpa got sick. I spent the years we were empty nesters taking care of him

Before The Flower Withers   by Dennis C Mariotis

until he died." Russ shook his head and said, "I think I get the picture. But didn't you and grandpa do anything during the years when you were raising your kids? Didn't you go on some nice vacations or anything like that?"

Rose walked to the kitchen table and sat down. She looked around the kitchen before answering him. Folding her hands she stared at the table and shook her head and said, "Not really. While your mom and your aunt were growing up, your great grandma and grandpa were also sick and needed help, and I was there for them too. Your grandpa worked two jobs to pay for all the bills and support his sick parents. With the exception of a few very short vacations, I was busy taking care of our daughters and his parents. Later on, I was very busy helping your mom and your aunt with their children. Then your grandpa passed away. Since my grandkids are grown up now, no one really needs me for anything."

Before The Flower Withers   *by Dennis C Mariotis*

Russ thought about all she said for a moment, then he shook his head and replied, "Sorry grandma, I didn't know that." Rose looked at him and grinned, "I love my family and I did what I had to do. So you see it's not the years in my life that I regret, it's the lack of life in my years that I lament. There were so many thrilling things that I wanted to do. Now that I have the money to do something exciting and only myself to take care of, I won't live long enough to get a chance to do anything."

Seeing Russ's disheartened expression, Rose realized he was feeling terrible for her. In an attempt to change the mood she forced a smile and apologized, "I'm sorry if I depressed you, honey. Forget the yard work! *Let the damn weeds grow!* Let's do something together today. I gotta get outta the house. How about taking in a movie? Or better yet, let's go to a ballgame! I hear the Yankees are in town!" Russ smiled, nodded and answered, "That's a great idea. We love baseball and I remember when you took

Before The Flower Withers   by Dennis C Mariotis

me to my first game. I'll put the mower away, go home and change my clothes, and I'll be back in an hour."

Studying Rose's body language and seeing that she looked tired and frustrated, Russ asked, "Are you sure you're up for it grandma?" Realizing that Russ picked up on her attempt at faking a good mood she quickly changed her expression. Then she smiled, winked, and answered, "I'm ready for anything!"

Russ thought for a moment trying to figure out what he could do for her for the little time remaining in her life. Hugging Rose, he let go, stepped back, and with a serious expression he stared her in the eyes. Before turning to leave he said, "Grandma? I want you to think about all the things you want to do, and when we get back from the ballgame, I want to sit down with you and make a list of what we can realistically do. I'm dedicating the next few months to spend my time, *only with you*, and having a lot of fun doing as many of those

Before The Flower Withers   *by Dennis C Mariotis*

things together!" This was very unexpected and hearing this lifted Rose out of her frustrated and depressed mood.

Seeing a huge smile on her face along with tears welling up in her eyes, Russ knew this was the best thing he could do for her. She hugged him tight, kissed his cheek, and her voice cracked as she replied, "I love you Russ. Thank you so much. I hope you know how happy you just made me! That's the best medicine I could've ever been prescribed! Now go home and change before this tough cookie goes to pieces and makes a mess of herself in front of you!"

Russ smiled at her and containing his emotions, he turned and quickly exited the house. Rose closed the door after he left, then leaned her back against the door and smiled as she wiped her eyes before walking out of the kitchen on her way to her bedroom where she changed clothes, and prepared for a fun day at the ballgame with Russ.

Before The Flower Withers   by Dennis C Mariotis

CHAPTER 3
Rose's Bucket List

Later on that afternoon Russ and Rose arrived home after they attended an Atlanta Braves, New York Yankees baseball game. Parking his car in her driveway, Russ then assisted Rose out of her seat. Arm in arm, together they walked up the porch steps to the front door of her house. Rose rummaged through her purse

Before The Flower Withers   by Dennis C Mariotis

for a moment but was unable to find her keys. Frustrated at herself she looked at Russ and exclaimed, "Damn it! I must have left my keys in the house!" Russ looked at her and said, "Don't worry grandma, my mom's got a spare key." Pointing at her rocking chair on her front porch he continued, "I'll go home and get it. Why don't you sit here and wait for me?"

Rose winked at Russ and replied, "I've got a better idea." With a surprised expression Russ asked, "You're not gonna break a window to get in, are you?" Shaking her head she answered, "Of course not!" Bending down in front of the door she lifted up the doormat with one hand and reached under it with her other hand. Standing up she looked at Russ and smiled as she held up a key and said, "There. I always keep a spare key under the mat."

Russ squinted his eyes and stared at her with a fearful expression of disbelief as he loudly exclaimed, "Grandma! You left the key to your house under the doormat?"

Before The Flower Withers   *by Dennis C Mariotis*

Rose's smile turned to a disappointed expression as she stared at him. She shook her head, pursed her lips, and said, "Well now that the whole neighborhood knows where I keep my spare key, I'll have to find a new hiding place!" Toning his voice down he said, "But that's so dangerous! Why even bother locking the door? Up until just now, I thought no one did that anymore!" With her hands on her hips she answered, "That key's been there for almost forty years and we've never had a problem!" Rose snickered then continued, "At this point, if someone came in and put me out of my misery, it wouldn't be a bad thing!"

Realizing her current condition and state of mind, Russ backed down and apologized, "I'm sorry grandma! But I would sleep a lot better at night if you let me find a better hiding place for the key, okay?" Smiling at him Rose replied, "That's okay honey. I'm glad you still worry and care a lot about me. I'm just afraid if we change the hiding place, I'll forget where it is!" Puzzled Russ

Before The Flower Withers   by Dennis C Mariotis

asked, "You remembered this hiding place for forty years, why do you think you'd forget a new one?" Rose grinned and answered, "Because my long term memory is great but my short term memory is horrible. Don't believe me? If you asked me who pitched for the Braves today, I'd probably tell you it was Warren Spahn!" They shared a hearty laugh, as they knew Warren Spahn's last year in major league baseball was in the mid 1960's.

Handing the spare key to Russ after opening the front door, Rose entered her house followed by Russ. Walking into the kitchen Russ sat down at the kitchen table. Rose walked to the sink area where she sat her handbag on the counter. Looking down where she placed her handbag she saw where she left her house keys and snickered saying, "There they are!" Russ looked over at her and seeing the keys he smiled. Rose opened a cabinet and took out two glasses. She placed them on the kitchen table and walked to the refrigerator where she opened the door, removed a two-liter bottle of soda, and

Before The Flower Withers   by Dennis C Mariotis

placed it on the table. She then walked into her living room for a moment and came back to the kitchen with a pad and pen in hand. Russ filled the glasses with soda while she was gone. Rose sat down at the table and placed the pad and pen in front of Russ.

    Russ took a minute to read what was written on the first page of the pad to himself. After he was done, he looked up at Rose and smiled saying, "I was only gone for an hour and you made this very long elaborate bucket list! That's very impressive!" Rose smiled at Russ and replied, "That's because I started writing that list over thirty years ago, and added to it ever since, up until the time your grandpa died. I took it out of my cedar chest today and blew the dust off of it." Russ looked at the list again, then looked at Rose and smiled. He replied, "Let's go down the list together and see what we can do within a reasonable time frame, okay grandma?" Rose nodded and smiled as she moved her chair around the table positioning it

Before The Flower Withers   by Dennis C Mariotis

next to Russ where they reviewed it together.

Before starting, Russ said, "Now I want you to choose the things that we can do within a three month period. I don't want you to pick things that are gonna tire you out so much that we have to stop, okay?" Rose nodded and replied, "I understand what you're saying and I know my limitations." Russ replied with kindness, "I'm sure you do. I want to do as much as we could do to make you as happy as possible. I just don't want you to be disappointed." Understanding his intentions, she put her arm around his shoulder and pulled him in for a hug as she kissed his cheek.

Turning their attention back to the pad he read it line by line aloud. As Russ read each item on the list they looked at each other. When they shook their heads, no, Russ crossed it off the list. When they nodded, he put a check mark by that line item. Looking through the list Russ and Rose laughed at some of the

Before The Flower Withers   by Dennis C Mariotis

things she listed. With a surprised expression on Russ' face, Rose shook her head 'no' when Russ asked, "Run with the bulls in Spain? You'll be trampled!" Reading further he was surprised and remarked, "Swim with the sharks?" To which Rose's reply made them laugh, "I'm safe. I read that sharks don't like old spoiled meat!" It took them about fifteen minutes to come up with a list of things they believed they could realistically do in a three month time frame.

Putting down the pad and pen, Russ rubbed his eyes. Turning to Rose he said, "That's a lot of things to do and I hope you're ready for 'em!" Rose shrugged her shoulders and smiling at him she replied, "I'm ready!" They grinned as they returned their attention to the list and studied it again. Russ then detached that sheet and put it to the side. On a clean sheet of paper he wrote down each item they agreed on. When he finished it, he showed the list to Rose who read through it and nodded her head saying, "Yeah. I think we can do all of them."

Before The Flower Withers   by Dennis C Mariotis

Looking at Russ she shrugged and said, "Well? Let's get started!"

On a neatly written page this is what she chose to do:

ROSE's BUCKET LIST:

- ✓ Do a modern day dance
- ✓ Sing karaoke
- ✓ Get Drunk.
- ✓ Go on a Police Ride Along
- ✓ Throw out the first ball at a baseball game
- ✓ Drive an Army Tank
- ✓ Gamble in Las Vegas
- ✓ Take a breath taking ride
- ✓ A day trip to France- have lunch & visit the Eifel Tower
- ✓ Ride on a Motorcycle
- ✓ Ride an Exotic Animal
- ✓ Climb a Mountain
- ✓ Get a Tattoo
- ✓ Change Someone's World
- ✓ Final wish is to be Cremated

Russ put the paper aside and stood up after he looked at the clock to check the time. He turned to Rose and said, "Mom and Aunt Helen will be here in about fifteen minutes. I better be going. I don't wanna be

Before The Flower Withers   by Dennis C Mariotis

around here when you break the news to them." Rose nodded and replied, "Go ahead. We'll meet again tomorrow morning and make our plans. I'm tired but I'm really excited about this. I know they're not all the great things I wanted to do but that's fine with me. The main thing is, I'm gonna be with someone I love while I'm doing them."

Russ couldn't hold in his emotions any longer as his eyes welled up with tears. He stood up and hugged Rose. Stepping back he choked back his tears and said, "I know and I wish we could do everything on your list together!" Rose smiled and said, "We could." With a puzzled expression Russ asked, "How?" Rose snickered as she answered, "We'll take a picture together on one of our trips. After I'm gone, take that picture of you and me and keep it with you everywhere you go." She chuckled then continued, "Except of course on your honeymoon."

Russ laughed and nodded, "It's a deal." Rose nodded as she smiled and pointed her finger in his

Before The Flower Withers   by Dennis C Mariotis

face, "And learn from this experience by making your own bucket list early in your life. Then go out and do all those glorious things you wanna do because when you get to my age it may be too late!" Russ smiled and replied, "I sure will grandma." She nodded, tilted her head and said, "I love you Russ." His lips quivered as he hugged her tightly and replied, "I love you too grandma!" He kissed her cheek before they parted. Russ nodded as he was unable to speak without breaking down. Then he turned and exited the kitchen and left her home. Rose sat down at the table and looked over the list. She wiped a tear from her eye then she looked up and smiled as she closed her eyes and imagined doing all the things on her list.

CHAPTER 4
The Fun Begins

"Are you ready grandma?" asked Russ as she opened the front door and let him in the house. Rose stood there dressed in her best outfit waiting for Russ. She was gleaming with excitement as she smiled and nodded. Seeing her Russ wolf whistled and said, "Well aren't you *the bomb*!" Confused at what he said Rose

Before The Flower Withers   by Dennis C Mariotis

inquired, "What's...*the bomb*?" Russ chuckled as he explained, "I believe your generation would say...*looking spiffy!*" Rose snickered and replied, "Now you're talking to where I can understand you. I've got a feeling there's gonna be a lot of things I'm gonna see that's changed between my generation and yours." Russ smiled as he replied, "Yep! From all the stories you told me I know that first hand. Well, it's almost six o'clock and we've gotta leave if we're gonna make it to Happy Hour at the bar in the club."

Rose shook her head as she picked up her purse and followed Russ out the door. While locking her front door she asked him, "What's so special about Happy Hour at the bar? I really don't drink so I don't know what that means." Walking arm and arm down the porch steps on their way to the waiting Uber cab Russ explained, "Grandma. When you told me you never got drunk before, I didn't think you meant you never had a buzz! Whoa! This is gonna be a real eye opening experience!" Confused, Rose inquired,

Before The Flower Withers   *by Dennis C Mariotis*

"What's a buzz? Is it the name of a cocktail?" Russ snickered as he replied, "You mean you really never had a drink before in your life?" She shook her head saying, "Your grandpa drank scotch and we always had a bottle or two in the house. One day I took a sip of his scotch and spit it out. It was nasty! I've been around drunk people and obviously I didn't like what I saw so I never cared for alcohol."

Before they entered the cab he asked, "Then why do you wanna get drunk?" Rose smiled as she replied, "Even though I didn't like what I saw in some of them...most of them looked like they were enjoying themselves...*a lot*. The quiet ones suddenly came to life and they were singing and dancing and walking into walls. The funny ones couldn't stop laughing. All of them came up to me and told me how much they loved me. Some of them sang the blues and cried. I'm curious to see what it's like and what I'm like in that state." Russ shook his head as he opened the car door and helped Rose into the back seat. After closing the door and

Before The Flower Withers   by Dennis C Mariotis

buckling their seat belts the cab drove off to the nightclub. Rose and everyone there were in for a treat.

Arriving at the club the cab stopped to let Rose and Russ out. After they exited the cab Rose stood there and looked at the club. Turning to him she said, "Russ. While we're out with your friends...please call me Rose, not grandma. Grandma sounds so old and tonight I wanna feel young again!" Russ smiled understanding where she was coming from and answered, "Okay gran...I mean *Rose*." Smiling and winking at her he offered his arm. She hooked his with hers and together they walked into the club.

Entering the club Rose looked around as Russ walked with her to the table where his friends were sitting. Most of his friends knew Rose and greeted her with respect. She said to all of them, "Now listen. I'm here to have a good time and I hope I don't cramp your style. So you do what you normally do and pretend like I'm one of your group. Okay?" They nodded except

Before The Flower Withers   by Dennis C Mariotis

for one young man who didn't know Rose. Turning to Russ he laughed and asked him, "Hey Russ! You trying to make it with the grandma type tonight?" Russ gave him a serious look and firmly replied, "I'm gonna let that slide tonight. Watch what you're saying. *She is* my *grandma*!" His friend was taken back with surprise and apologized, "Sorry man, I didn't know."

A couple of minutes went by and a waitress came to their table. She asked, "What's everybody gonna have tonight?" Russ's friends ordered and when it came Rose's turn she looked at Russ and shrugged. Russ ordered for her, "Give her a Harvey Wallbanger." She asked, "What's that?" The waitress replied, "It's a drink mixed with orange juice." Rose smiled and said, "I love orange juice! I guess it can't be that bad!" The people at the table laughed at her comment.

Within a few minutes the waitress came back to their table with their drinks. Distributing them to everyone she served Rose's two glasses

Before The Flower Withers   by Dennis C Mariotis

last, "And you have the Harvey Wallbangers." Rose looked around and asked, "Why did you give me two when everyone else got one?" The waitress explained, "Everyone else ordered shots so we doubled their drinks and used one glass. This is Happy Hour and all drinks are two for one. I'll come by shortly to see if you want a refill. Enjoy!" Rose nodded to the waitress.

Holding his glass up, Russ made a toast. "Here's to Rose's first drink!" They all smiled and took a drink. Rose took a long gulp and immediately put her glass down and gasped for air for a couple of seconds. Russ looked at her with concern and said, "Are you all right Rose?" Unable to speak momentarily Rose nodded. Regaining her composure she placed her hand across her chest and said, "Yeah. I'm all right. I just never drank such strong orange juice." Then another person at the table made another toast, "To Rose and many more glasses of strong orange juice!" Rose smiled, took a deep breath and along with everyone she took another large gulp. After

Before The Flower Withers   by Dennis C Mariotis

putting her glass down on the table her sour face turned into a smile. Then she raised her glass and drank the rest of her drink in several straight gulps. Putting her glass down she blinked several times and let out a sound of enjoyment, "Ah. I think I'm starting to acquire a taste for this."

Licking her lips Rose picked up her other glass and took a big gulp. When she placed her glass down she looked at Russ and smiled, "I didn't know what I was missing all these years. Order me a couple more, will you dear?" Looking around at the others she noticed the table was quiet and they were all staring at her with disbelief. Russ whispered to her, "Rose: I think you better take it slow and pace yourself." She looked at him, nodded, and said, "I think you're right. Things are starting to look funny."

Just as Rose was finishing her second drink a man in his sixties approached the table and stopped. Looking at her he asked,

Before The Flower Withers   by Dennis C Mariotis

"Excuse me pretty lady but would you like to dance?" She looked at Russ. Nudging her arm Russ said to her, "Go ahead Rose. This is one of the things on your list. Later on they'll have Karaoke. We just might get three items checked off tonight!" She nodded and looked at the man as she scooted out of the booth, "Come on Romeo. I always wanted to learn a dance to the music of this generation. Let's show these kids how it's done!"

Rose and the man walked up to the dance floor. They were the only ones dancing to the modern day rap song the best that they could. Within a few minutes they were joined by eight other young couples who were doing more modern dance moves. After watching the other couples, Rose's partner mimicked them as he danced around her. When he got behind her he put his hands on her waist and pulled her to where her backside was up against his groin. Rose quickly pulled his hands off her, stepped forward, and turned around. She gave the man the most hateful and disgusted look she could, and then she

Before The Flower Withers   by Dennis C Mariotis

walked off the dance floor and back to the table.

With an angry expression she turned to Russ and said, "Did you see what that pervert tried to do? And right on the dance floor in front of everyone?" Russ' friends covered their faces with their hands to keep her from seeing them laughing. Russ said, "Rose? You were the one who said you wanted to do a more modern dance to this music. Look at those other couples on the dance floor!" She turned and looked. A horrified expression came over her. With her mouth and eyes wide open she turned to Russ and said, *"What the hell are they doing?"* With embarrassment in his voice, Russ explained, "Rose. That dance is called The Bump and Grind."

His friends tried even harder to contain their laughter behind their covered mouths when they heard Rose's angry reply as she shook her head in disgust, *"That's what my generation did in private! Only we called it...dry humping!"* Russ chuckled when Rose leaned towards him and

Before The Flower Withers   by Dennis C Mariotis

quietly said, "*You can check **that** shit off my list!*" Stopping the waitress as she walked by, Rose requested, "*I'll have another Harvey Wallplaster please!*" The waitress snickered and with a confused expression asked Rose, "Never heard of that. Did you mean Wallbanger?" Rose smiled and nodded.

Finishing up her sixth drink about two hours later, Rose was beginning to feel the full effects of the liquor. Her face also showed that she was under the influence. She began to slur her words as she conversed with Russ, "Russs, I think I fffinnally know what gettin' a buzzz ffffeels like. I think itsabuzzz! Anyway, I really love you Russss! And ahm ready to do krapioki!" This brought a round of laughter from the others at the table. Rose even broke out into a silly laugh, "I guessss I must-ov said sssomething fffunny!"

Russ looked at her and said, "You've had quite a bit to drink. Are you sure that's such a good idea?" Rose looked at him, straightened up and

Before The Flower Withers   by Dennis C Mariotis

said, "Ahm okay, and I better do it now before I lose my nerve." She rubbed her eyes and spoke more soberly saying, "Ahm gonna sing the song I sang at grandpa's funeral. The name of it is *'I Will Always Love You,'* and then ahm gonna sing a lively song named *'Twist And Shout'*."

Scooting across and exiting the booth Rose walked through the crowd and up to the DJ. When she finished speaking to him, he handed her a piece of paper and had her write the songs she wanted to sing. Handing it back to him after she wrote down the songs, she took her place in line as she sat down in the fourth seat waiting for her turn.

During the time they waited for Rose to sing, Russ explained to his friends about Rose's condition and that this was part of her bucket list. This made them more eager and very glad to be a part of this memorable time for their friend Russ as well as Rose. When it came her turn to sing, Russ and his friends cheered and

Before The Flower Withers   by Dennis C Mariotis

whistled for her when the DJ announced, "We have a special treat tonight. Our next singer is a beautiful young lady named Rose and she's gonna sing two songs for you. And here she is... Rose!"

Standing up Rose felt the butterflies in her stomach. She was always nervous anytime she was in front of an audience. Walking up to the stage she looked at everyone. Standing on stage with everyone watching her temporarily sobered her up. Silence came over the crowd as she spoke to them with honesty and sincerity in her voice, "Thank you for the warm greeting. You see, tonight is a very special night. A week ago I was told I have terminal cancer and I have about six months left." You could have heard a pin drop. Everyone stopped including the workers. All eyes were on Rose. Waving to Russ she continued, "My handsome grandson over there helped me make out my bucket list. Karaoke is just one of the things on my list. I want to dedicate this song to him."

Before The Flower Withers   by Dennis C Mariotis

Turning to the DJ she said, "I'm ready."

The music began. After the song's intro, Rose began to sing. She had a beautiful voice and sang the song with feeling and emotion. The crowd watched in amazement at Rose's courage and talent. She went on and finished the song in great style. When she was done there was *NOT* a dry eye in the house as the crowd's cheers went on for almost two minutes. People wiped their eyes as they clapped, cheered and whistled. Even the two muscle bound doorman bouncers wiped their eyes and cheered.

Drying her eyes, Rose bowed and thanked the crowd. She paused for a moment, then spoke, "Thank you. I had to get that out of my system. For my next song I want to pick up the tempo and celebrate going out of this life in style and I want everybody to get up and dance." Turning to the DJ she shouted, *"Hit it big boy!"*

The DJ pressed the play button and the music began. Rose picked

Before The Flower Withers   by Dennis C Mariotis

up the mood. Everyone laughed and danced as they enjoyed her rendition of *'Twist and Shout'*. She was great on stage as she walked and skipped around the stage singing like a young music star. At one point Rose put her hand under her blouse and behind her back. Surprising everyone she undid her bra, pulled it off and out from under her blouse and waved it around as she sang and danced. This brought roaring laughter and cheers from the crowd. Swinging it around she threw it into the crowd on the dance floor in front of her.

When she was done, she bowed and thanked everyone again before leaving the stage. After she stepped down from the stage she was greeted by a long line of people who shook her hand, hugged her, kissed her cheek, and gave her words of encouragement. When she reached the booth Russ stood there with streaks of tears running down his face along with his friends as they all hugged her.

Before The Flower Withers   *by Dennis C Mariotis*

As she went to sit down she laughed when she noticed there were twelve Harvey Wallbangers waiting for her. Turning to Russ she said, "Thanks honey!" Russ replied, "That's not from me! That's from all your adoring fans!" Rose turned around and blew kisses to everyone who was still clapping for her.

Sitting down Rose let out a huge sigh of relief and said, "Wow! That was exhilarating! And I'm really thirsty." Then she reached over and chugged one of her drinks. Russ gently patted her on the back and said, "That was incredible Rose. And I can't believe you took your bra off and threw it!" They all laughed. With curiosity in his voice one of the guys at the table asked, "Yeah! But after you did that what were those things sticking out of your blouse near your waist?" Russ' eyes widened as he glared at his friend and shook his head. Rose laughed hysterically as did everyone at the table when she answered, "I'm a seventy five year old lady. What did you think they were?...*My boobs!*" Picking up

Before The Flower Withers   by Dennis C Mariotis

another glass Rose gulped it down almost as quickly as the previous one.

Arriving at Rose's house later that night after the club, Russ exited the Uber cab along with the driver. Russ, assisted by the driver, helped Rose out of the cab. With an arm around each guy's shoulder, they helped walk Rose, who was stone drunk up the porch steps. As they walked her she was slur-singing the songs she sang earlier during her turn at Karaoke up the steps and into the house. After exiting the house the Uber driver laughed all the way back to his car as he could still hear Rose's singing coming from inside her home.

Inside Rose's house, she sat on the bathroom floor next to the toilet. Outside the bathroom Russ sat on a chair watching her. Russ asked her, "Grandma, are you all right?" Rose opened her eyes and staring at Russ she blinked a few times, smiled, and answered, "Yeah. I'm fine Russ, Russ, and Russ." Russ squinted and asked, "What?" Smiling she chuckled, "I'm

Before The Flower Withers   by Dennis C Mariotis

answering all three of you!" Making a familiar face Russ recognized the expression just as Rose said, "But I think I'm gonna get sick. Where's the toilet?" Russ stood up and answered, "You're sitting next to it."

Rose had the presence of mind to shut the door. The sound of Rose throwing up in the bathroom made Russ cringe and shake his head. Standing next to the bathroom door he asked, "Are you all right grandma?" It took a couple of seconds for Rose to respond, "I'm all right. I had to hold onto the toilet bowl to stop it from spinning around. It looks like a giant Margarita." Russ snickered saying, "Don't lick the sides, it's not salt." Hearing that made her upchuck again. For the next ten minutes Rose threw up everything she had in her system. When she was done, Russ helped clean her up along with cleaning the bathroom. Then he helped her up and walked her over to her couch where he laid her down on her stomach. Tuffy, her cat, climbed on the top of the couch until he reached the top of the backrest above Rose's head

Before The Flower Withers   by Dennis C Mariotis

where he sprawled out and fell asleep. Russ stayed awake the rest of the night monitoring Rose.

When Rose woke up the next morning she saw Russ sitting in front of her. Sitting up she grabbed her head with both hands and rocked back and forth, "I feel awful. What an experience. So that's what getting drunk and having a good time is like. I don't ever wanna do that again!" Russ handed her a cup of coffee. He smiled and chuckled, "For someone who never drank before, you sure tied one on. I thought I was gonna have to have your stomach pumped!"

Rose thought a moment as she sipped the coffee, and with an agonizing expression she tried to smile as she asked, "Did I make a fool out of myself last night?" Russ shook his head and said, "Well there was that one time when you told my friends at the table those limericks you heard from grandpa." Hearing that made Rose cringe as she put her head down onto her hand. Looking back up at Russ she asked, "Oh

Before The Flower Withers   *by Dennis C Mariotis*

I hope it wasn't the one about…" Nodding his head Russ smiled as he interrupted her, "Yes it was! Let's see, there once was a man from Nantucket…" Rose put her hand up and laughed as she interrupted Russ, "Oh no! Why didn't you stop me?" Russ put his hands up and shrugged as if he surrendered and answered, "Oh I tried but my friends wanted to hear all of them. Eventually I got you to stop." Rose shook her head and replied, "I guess your friends think I'm a crazy old lunatic?" Russ proudly smiled and answered, "No way! They think you're the coolest grandma in the world. They want you to come out with us the next time we go out! Just do me one favor please?" Curious, Rose asked, "What's that?" Russ answered, "I know how much you love limericks but if you're ever out with me again and you have a few Harvey Wallplasters, like you kept calling them, don't tell any more nasty limericks! Deal?" Rose smiled and replied, "Deal!"

Rose rubbed her temples and thought for a moment. She snickered

Before The Flower Withers   by Dennis C Mariotis

asking, "Outside of the limericks, did I do anything else foolish?" Russ smiled proudly again as he answered, "Grandma. You were great. Everybody loved you. You made them cry and you made them laugh and I got pictures. All except for the time that guy tried to bump and grind with you!" Rose shook her head and with a disgusted expression she said, "That's the one thing I remember! But what I don't remember, is what the hell happened to my bra?" Russ shook his head and answered, "When you were singing 'Twist and Shout' you went into wild woman mode and took it off. Then you swung it around and around over your head before throwing it out to the crowd!" She gasped and then she laughed hysterically as she clapped her hands and replied, "Holy shit! I don't remember that. I'm so glad you told me because I was afraid to ask you about it!" Shaking her head she continued, "How many items from the list did we accomplish?" Russ answered, "Three."

Russ took out his cell phone and showed her the pictures. Rose

Before The Flower Withers   by Dennis C Mariotis

```
and Russ pointed, laughed and talked
about the events of that night. After
Russ put his cell phone away he sat
down next to Rose and went over the
next things to do on her list.
```

Before The Flower Withers   by Dennis C Mariotis

CHAPTER 5
The Police Ride Along

`The next bucket list` item Rose and Russ decided on was to go on a police ride along. This is where a civilian is allowed to accompany the police in their cruiser during an actual patrol. Rose's son-in-law, Joe, is a Deputy Sherriff with the Cobb County Sherriff's department. Russ called and spoke with his uncle the next day. Special consideration was

Before The Flower Withers   *by Dennis C Mariotis*

given to Rose due to her health which sped up the approval for her to ride with her son-in-law.

Two days later we find Rose riding in the backseat of a police cruiser in the early morning hours of the third shift. Her son-in-law, Deputy Joe, is driving. Sitting in the front passenger seat accompanying them is his partner Deputy Nancy.

It was a very uneventful night up until about 2:30 a.m. That's when the excitement started. Rose was startled by the sudden sound of the police car's radio as it came to life. A couple of loud beeps caught the officers' attention as they leaned closer to hear the Dispatcher. The sudden excitement caused Rose a rush of adrenalin which made her snap up in her seat and look around. With all the excitement Rose leaned forward to hear everything.

The message from the police Dispatcher came over the radio, "Attention. We have a 10-65 reported at Justin's Food Mart located at 621 Main.

Before The Flower Withers   by Dennis C Mariotis

The suspect fled the scene on foot. The suspect is described as a male Caucasian wearing blue jeans, a red Atlanta Braves hoodie, and white tennis shoes. He's armed and dangerous." Cringing after listening to the message Rose exclaimed, "Oh damn!" Deputy Joe picked up the radio's microphone but before answering the Dispatcher about the call, he checked on Rose. With a firm concerned tone, "What's the matter Rose?" Shaking her head as she answered Joe, in a very frustrated tone she replied, *"What's this world coming to? Did he have to be a Braves' fan? I'd feel so much better if he was a Yankee fan!* By the way, what's a 10-65?"

Looking at Deputy Nancy who had her hand over her mouth as she snickered under her breath, Joe shrugged as he slightly turned his head towards Rose in the back seat and snickered saying, "He's probably a Yankee fan disguised as a Braves fan!" This made Rose feel better as she nodded and smiled. Putting the radio's microphone up to his mouth Joe answered the Dispatcher while Nancy worked the

Before The Flower Withers   by Dennis C Mariotis

cruiser's lights and sirens. He replied, "Car 47, Officers Gardner and Fresco responding to the 10-65. We're headed south on Main and should arrive within one minute." The Dispatcher immediately responded, "Roger that Car 47. Approach with extreme caution! Backup is five minutes away!"

Deputy Nancy quickly turned to address Rose's question and to instruct her on what to do in this situation. Speaking in a firm tone, "Miss Miles; A 10-65 is police code for an armed robbery. In this case the person was reported to be armed with a gun and very dangerous. For your safety and ours you will remain in the car at all times. Do you understand?" Rose nodded and answered, "Yes and please call me Rose. But what if I have to go to the bathroom? I mean all this excitement is upsetting my system." Deputy Nancy answered, "Rose. This is a very serious and dangerous situation. Please remain calm and hold it. When it's over we'll get you to a bathroom immediately. Okay?" Rose nodded and said, "I'll do my best."

Before The Flower Withers   by Dennis C Mariotis

A couple of blocks before the crime scene Deputy Joe spotted a man matching the suspect walking on the sidewalk toward the police car. When the man saw the police car, he turned around and walked in the opposite direction. Pulling over to confront the man Officer Joe stopped the car. He reached up with his right hand and turned off the interior lighting so as not to illuminate the inside of the cruiser when they opened the doors.

Officer Nancy immediately opened her door and hastily exited the car where she kneeled down shielding herself behind the car's front right fender with her revolver pointed at the suspect. With his revolver in hand Officer Joe rolled down his window, reached out, and turned the car's spot light on him. When the light shined the officers clearly saw the man wearing a red Braves hoodie and blue jeans. Just as Joe opened his door and kneeled down behind it with his gun also pointed at the suspect, Officer Nancy yelled,

Before The Flower Withers   by Dennis C Mariotis

"Police! Freeze and put your hands on your head!" Hearing this, the suspect bolted and ran into an alley between two buildings.

Seeing him take off, both officers ran after him. During their run, Officer Nancy used her shoulder radio to call the Dispatcher to report they were actively chasing after a male Caucasian that matched the description of the suspect as well as their location. The Officers approached the alley with extreme caution. Officer Joe pointed his flashlight down the alley while Officer Nancy pointed her gun in that direction to cover him. They waited long enough to see that the suspect was nowhere in sight. They waited two more minutes hoping the suspect would come out of hiding, but to no avail. They lost him.

Meanwhile Rose sat quietly in the back seat of the car as she was instructed. She was a bit nervous, as she was alone in the dark. She kept a watchful eye as she vigilantly looked around the streets.

Before The Flower Withers   by Dennis C Mariotis

With the driver's side door open she was able to hear the sounds outside of the car. Suddenly she heard footsteps approaching from her left. Looking out the window, with the aid of the moonlight, she was able to make out a figure standing at the edge of the building peeking down the street to where Officers Joe and Nancy were located. Since there was nothing blocking the backseat of the cruiser from the front seat, Rose leaned forward and was able to reach the shotgun in the front area. She managed to pull it out of the holder without making a sound. Feeling safer now she watched the dark figure as she quietly sat in the back seat cradling the shotgun.

  Rose's eyes grew wider when she saw the figure slowly approach the police cruiser. She swallowed hard and became very nervous as the figure, now crouched down and slowly coming closer. Suddenly the figure hastened his pace and within a couple of seconds he entered the front of the cruiser and sat in the driver's seat.

Before The Flower Withers   by Dennis C Mariotis

Not wanting to make any noise the stranger didn't close the door as he first reached for the keys in the ignition. Finding them there he said in a low voice to himself, "Thanks for the ride you dumb pigs." Just before he turned the keys the man froze as he was startled by the sound that came from the backseat of the cruiser. It was the unmistakable sound of someone chambering a shotgun shell into a shotgun's barrel. Overcome with fear from this surprise, his eyes and mouth widened when he felt the cold steel from the business end of the shotgun barrel against his neck.

With a firm stern voice he heard Rose say, *"Okay dirt-bag! Put your hands on your head and don't move or I'll blow your head off!"* Thinking it was a police officer in the backseat, the man put his hands on his head as instructed. In a nervous tone the man pleaded, **"Okay! Okay! You got me. Don't shoot!"** Rose continued, "Now, really slow! I want you to keep one hand on your head and blow the horn and hold it down with the other. When my

Before The Flower Withers   by Dennis C Mariotis

backup gets here you will stop blowing the horn and put your hand back on your head. *Remember... real slow!"*

Backing away from the alley and out of harm's way the officers called the Dispatcher to give an update on their progress. Officer Joe reported, "Officer Gardner reporting on the 10-65." The Dispatcher replied, "Go ahead." Officer Joe continued, "Pursued the suspect on foot. We lost him down a dark alley on Main between 8th and 9th. We're waiting for backup before continuing." The Dispatcher replied, "Roger. Remain cautious. Backup is one minute away."

Just as the Dispatcher finished, the officers heard a car horn continuously blowing. Officer Joe looked at Officer Nancy and with a surprised look his eyes widened as he said, **"Rose!"** The officers quickly turned and ran as fast as they could towards their cruiser while holding their pistols pointed up. Officer Joe signaled his partner to slow down when he saw someone in the front seat of his

Before The Flower Withers   by Dennis C Mariotis

cruiser. They momentarily stopped just as their backup in the form of two additional police cruisers arrived and stopped. They waited for their fellow officers to exit their cars. Using their radios they communicated to one another regarding the situation.

      They slowly approached the cruiser and surrounded it with their guns pointed at the man in the front seat. Walking closer Officer Joe commanded, "Put your hands outside of the car where I can see them!" The man answered, "I can't. The person behind me ordered me to keep them on my head!" Walking closer to the car the officer noticed the man had his hands folded on top of his head. Officer Joe held his gun pointed at the man and squinted into the car. With a puzzled expression he addressed his fellow officers, "Hold your fire everyone!" The officers surrounding the car watched and pointed their guns up as Officer Joe requested. Speaking into the cruiser he questioned, "Rose? Is that you?"

Before The Flower Withers   by Dennis C Mariotis

Within a couple of seconds he heard Rose answer, "Yes it's me. Don't shoot!" All the officers chuckled when Rose, while holding the shotgun against the man's neck, reached up and turned on the interior light. She looked at Joe and smiling she said, "I was holding him for you and I stayed in the car like I was told to do!" Looking in the rear view mirror the suspect was surprised to see an old lady holding the shotgun and frowning at him. With a look of disgust he asked Officer Joe, "Who is she?" Joe smiled and said, "She's my mother-in-law! And you're lucky she didn't blow your head off for wearing that Braves hoodie!" Rose chimed in, *"Yeah! Shame on you!"*

Two of the officers who arrived as backup took the criminal out of Officer Joe's cruiser. Frisking him they found the gun he used in the armed robbery. Then they handcuffed him and after reading him his Miranda rights they placed him in the back of their car and drove him to jail. Afterwards, Officers Joe and Nancy drove Rose home.

Before The Flower Withers   by Dennis C Mariotis

CHAPTER 6
Hey Ump! You're Out!

The next day, Rose was visited by the news media. Reporters from the local television news as well as the local newspaper interviewed her and broadcasted her heroic story. Rose told reporters in detail all the events that led up to her capturing that dangerous criminal. The reporters nicknamed her '*Shotgun Grandma Rose*' in their stories. People came from all around the area to thank

Before The Flower Withers   by Dennis C Mariotis

her and take pictures with her for their social media page.

After coming home at almost four o'clock in the morning, and staying awake throughout most of the next day due to the attention and notoriety she received, Rose was exhausted. She was feeling the fatigue described by Dr. Bill. It took her a couple of days of rest to recover.

A few days later she received a call from Russ. He wanted to make sure she was well rested before he came to see her. She was excited because he told her he had some incredible news for her. When she asked what it was he wouldn't tell her. The only thing he said was that this was something he wanted to show her and tell her in person. She told him to come over right away. Hanging up the phone Rose rushed to shower and change her clothes.

About an hour later Russ pulled up in her driveway. With an envelope under his arm, he exited his car, walked up to the front door, and

Before The Flower Withers   by Dennis C Mariotis

rang the bell. Rose saw him coming and immediately opened the door, "Hey honey. Come in and sit down." Walking into the house Russ greeted her saying, "Hey grandma!" Then he gave her a hug and a kiss on the cheek. She reciprocated. Taking a seat on the sofa Russ held the envelope in his hands and grinned as he waited for Rose to take a seat next to him.

       Holding the envelope out for Rose to see it, she smiled and said, "Ooo! It's from the Atlanta Braves and it's got my name on it! Is it an autographed team picture?" Russ nodded and smiled, "Uh huh! But there's more. A lot more! Guess!" Scratching her head Rose thought for a minute, then guessed, "Tickets for the rest of the season?" She looked at Russ. He smiled and said, "Yeah. And there's one more thing!" Rose stared off and thought for a moment. Since nothing else came to her mind, they laughed at her silly guess, "Harvey Wallbangers for life?" Russ shook his head, *"Nooo! Give up?"* Shrugging her shoulders Rose answered, "Yeah!"

Before The Flower Withers   by Dennis C Mariotis

Russ opened the envelope as Rose sat excited with anticipation at the contents. Pulling out the autographed team photo and handing it to her, she smiled as she took it and gazed at it, then pulling out a pair of season ticket passes behind home plate made her even more excited. Placing his hand in the envelope he pulled out a letter. Rose waited with baited breath as Russ held it up to read it to her. He said, "This is a special gift for you. Ready?" With a big smile Rose answered, "Yeah!"

As he read the letter Rose had a burst of energy and excitement. She looked and listened with her hands folded under her chin, and a huge smile on her face. Clearing his throat Russ read:

"Dear Rose Miles.

The Atlanta Braves organization wishes to congratulate you for the bravery you displayed in risking your life for the citizen's of Cobb County by single handedly capturing a dangerous criminal. We are also very proud that

Before The Flower Withers   by Dennis C Mariotis

you are also a huge fan of our ballclub. In addition to the enclosed autographed team photo and season tickets, we request the honor of your presence at this Saturday's game and invite you to be our special guest where we will commemorate your incredibly brave deed by having you throw out the first ball. Please contact our General Manager at the phone number listed below with your response. We're looking forward to sharing this moment with you. It's fans like you that make our community great!"

Rose jumped up, laughed out loud, and clapped her hands as she hopped up and down like a schoolgirl. With an excited tone she said, "YEAH! WOW! I can't believe it!" Shaking her head at Russ who smiled as he watched her reaction, she toned it down and asked, "How did this happen?" Russ smiled answering, "I spoke to Uncle Joe and told him about your Bucket List. The Public Relations person from the Cobb County Sherriff's department contacted the Braves' office and the

Before The Flower Withers   *by Dennis C Mariotis*

Braves approved it. You're a hometown hero grandma!"

Rose shook her head and said, "That's so cool!" She thought for a second then looked at Russ and smiling she said, "You know what I'm gonna do?" Russ shrugged his shoulders and shook his head, "No. What're you gonna do?" Nodding, Rose grinned as she answered, "I'm gonna go down to the jailhouse and give that crook a big sloppy kiss! If it wasn't for him, all this wouldn't have happened!" Russ shook his head as he replied, "I don't think that's such a good idea grandma! That guy vowed revenge on you!" Rose snickered saying, "Well I'm still so pissed off at him for dishonoring my favorite team by wearing that shirt, that I might just kick his butt, after I kissed him!" Russ and Rose laughed as he handed her the letter. Rose looked at it and shook her head as she read it to herself. After taking a couple of hours with Rose that afternoon, Russ left and went home.

Before The Flower Withers   by Dennis C Mariotis

The next morning, Rose called Russ and requested him to come early so she could warm up her arm and practice throwing by playing catch with him. She wanted to make that first pitch as perfect as possible. She waited for him at the far end of her driveway with two baseball gloves and baseballs as Russ pulled into her driveway. Walking up to him after he exited his car Rose handed him a glove and said, "Hey honey. Thanks for doing this." Taking the glove and putting it on his hand Russ winked at Rose and replied, "Anything for you grandma. This is gonna be a very memorable occasion! Are ya' ready?" Putting on her glove and punching the glove's pocket she gritted her teeth and replied, "I was born ready!"

The two separated as they walked backwards until they reached about the distance between the pitcher's mound and home plate. Rose did her best imitation of a major league pitcher as she wound up and threw the ball to Russ. It was high and wide but slow enough for Russ to react

Before The Flower Withers   by Dennis C Mariotis

and catch it. Rose yelled, "Sorry honey!" Russ replied, "That's okay grandma. You have good form and decent speed. Just aim at my glove." Rose shook her head. Picking up another baseball she wound up and pitched again. This time it was faster and went over Russ' head and wide to the left. Russ yelled, "Take it easy grandma. Don't rush." The next pitch was much better. Russ nodded before throwing the ball back to her.

This went on for about twenty minutes before Rose made the time out sign to Russ. Walking to him, Russ saw that she was huffing and puffing. With concern in his voice he asked, "You're really out of breath. Are you okay?" Between deep breaths Rose puffed answering, "Yeah! I'm okay. I just get a lot more tired these days after doing simple things." Russ grinned and nodded but didn't say anything. He was trying to keep calm after he remembered what Dr. Bill told Rose in his office that day after Rose asked him about the symptoms to expect when the end was close.

Before The Flower Withers   *by Dennis C Mariotis*

      Collecting the gloves and baseballs they walked inside her house. Russ waited while Rose cleaned up and changed her clothes for the game. Walking into the living room Russ smiled when he saw what she was wearing. She stood there as Russ admired her outfit. She had on an Atlanta Braves hat and a game jersey, along with a light blue pair of blue jeans and white sneakers. When she turned around Russ chuckled, "That's great!" when he saw it. On the back of her jersey she had her age, 75, and over her age she had her first name in capitals 'ROSE'. Turning around and picking up her purse, Rose gave him a high five as she walked passed him and exited her house. Russ exited after her and locked the door on his way out.

      Arriving two hours early Rose and Russ were greeted by security at the stadium's VIP parking entrance. Showing their passes they let them in to park their car and enter the stadium. There they met with the club's Public Relations team who led them on a short tour before sitting them down and

Before The Flower Withers   by Dennis C Mariotis

explaining the details of the tradition of throwing out the first ball. After that they were walked out to the dugout where they met the players. They were having a fantastic time as the players were perfect professionals and treated them great. They laughed and joked when they spoke to Rose about her heroic deed and all the players signed the back of her jersey. They gave her and Russ autographed bats and baseballs. A newspaper reporter was there taking pictures and writing notes for an exclusive story in the sports section.

The time passed quickly and it was time for Rose to take the mound and throw out the ceremonial first pitch. She walked out of the dugout accompanied by the club's personnel. The stadium was almost full with cheering fans. Reaching the pitcher's mound, Rose waited for the stadium announcer. Then his voice came over the stadium speakers, "Attention ladies and gentlemen." The crowd quieted down and watched the event on the field as he continued, "Throwing out this game's first pitch is a very

Before The Flower Withers   by Dennis C Mariotis

special person. She's a local hero named Rose Miles." The announcer briefly paused as the crowd responded with low level clapping and cheering. Then the crowd came to life and gave her a deafening standing roaring ovation when the announcer continued, "She's better known as, *Shotgun Grandma Rose!*"

Seeing the crowd come to life, Rose took off her hat and tipped it to the crowd as she turned to everyone around the stadium and blew all of them kisses with her other hand. The clapping continued but the cheering level lowered as the crowd sat down and waited for Rose to throw out the ceremonial first pitch.

The club representative handed Rose a baseball. She brought a thunderous roar of laughter and smiles from the fans and players when she went through the motions of acting like a major league pitcher by holding her glove under her arm as she took the ball and rubbed it hard with both hands. Then she scratched herself and

Before The Flower Withers   by Dennis C Mariotis

spit on the ground before stepping on the pitcher's mound. The laughter and cheering increased when she bent down and looked at the catcher. She stared at him and shook her head as if she was shaking off the catcher's sign. Two seconds later she nodded at the catcher. Taking a full wind up she reared back and threw a perfect strike!

The crowd came back to life. They stood and cheered very loud. Then the crowd went into a chant. In unison they yelled, "Throw one more! Throw one more! Throw one more!" With all the noise the Public Relations Director smiled and nodded as he handed Rose another baseball. Rose took it, smiled and waved to the crowd. Then she went back into her major league pitcher act. After looking at the catcher and nodding she reared back and threw the ball. With her adrenaline flowing from the reaction of the crowd to a great first pitch, Rose threw this pitch faster.

Unfortunately this pitch was wild and way off the catcher's

Before The Flower Withers   by Dennis C Mariotis

glove target. The home plate umpire who was standing about ten feet away was talking to a player and was not paying attention. The baseball headed straight at him. Seeing this Rose, Russ, and all the players near the umpire yelled, "Look out!" Hearing this and caught totally by surprise the umpire looked in Rose's direction just as the ball came screaming at him. *Pow!* The ball hit the umpire on the bridge of his nose and between his eyes. He went down like he was shot. The crowd noise went from cheering to a dead silence as they watched the medics along with Rose rush to the fallen umpire.

Rose and Russ were escorted off the field and into the dugout where they spent the rest of the game with the players. After a forty-minute delay for the umpire's medical attention, the game started. In the dugout some of the players congratulated Rose on hitting the umpire. One pitcher walked up to her and said, "Thanks Rose. I wanted to do that two weeks ago when he called a game that I pitched. He missed so many

Before The Flower Withers   by Dennis C Mariotis

strike calls. Then he threw me out of the game for arguing with him!" Rose sat on the bench with an apologetic smile and replied, "I saw that game and I was really angry at him, but what I did was an accident. I hope he's gonna be okay."

The pitcher nodded and snickered as he replied, "You sure did a good job when you beaned him! He's got a broken nose and a couple of black eyes. He looks like a giant raccoon umpire with a bad sinus problem. Maybe you did him big a favor!" With a puzzled look Rose asked, "For a minute, I thought I killed him. How did I do him a big favor?" The pitcher chuckled before walking away as he answered, "You might have straightened out his eye sight. I'm on the mound tomorrow. Maybe now he'll be able to see the strikes I throw!" Rose and Russ shook their heads and snickered.

Before The Flower Withers   by Dennis C Mariotis

CHAPTER 7
Rose Drives A Tank

A few days after the baseball game, Russ met with Rose at her house to discuss their next adventure. They sat at the kitchen table as they went through the list. Taking a short break Rose stood up and walked to the kitchen counter where she took the carafe containing fresh brewed coffee and refilled their coffee mugs

Before The Flower Withers   by Dennis C Mariotis

before returning it to the coffee-maker. Returning to her seat at the table she was excited and looking forward to the next item. Putting her bucket-list down Russ smiled as he looked at Rose and said, "I really enjoyed the ballgame. We've got the letter from Fort Benning approving your ride in an army tank yesterday. They state it's absolutely safe since they use a tank that's mechanically disarmed for battle and that it's only used for teaching soldiers how to drive."

Rose smiled and nodded, "I can hardly wait! Are you gonna be in the tank with me?" Russ shook his head and with a serious expression answered, "Are you kidding me? After what you did to that umpire? No way!" They both laughed. Rose looked on as Russ picked up the letter and pointed to it as he read it to her, "See here grandma? It states 'this is a fifteen minute tour allowing the civilian named above,' that's you, 'to participate in a field operation of a military armored vehicle.' After what happened to the umpire, I'm gonna take my chances

Before The Flower Withers   by Dennis C Mariotis

watching you from a distance." Rose looked at him and replied, "I think you'll be safer."

Finishing their coffee they continued their conversation. They laughed and joked with each other. It was about two o'clock in the afternoon when Russ decided to leave. Standing Russ said, "Grandma. I've gotta go home and get some things ready for tomorrow." Rose also stood and letting out a short groan she replied, "Yeah and I've got to get some rest." Russ studied her expression after he heard her groan and seeing her cringe for a couple of seconds concerned him. He asked, "Are you in any pain?" Rose grinned as she answered, "Oh you know. It comes with everything I'm going through. I took the meds Dr. Bill gave me. I'll be fine."

Not satisfied with her response, Russ pressed her, "Are you sure? I mean, we can call this off until you're feeling better!" Trying to reassure him, Rose shook her head and snickered as she answered, "I'm having

Before The Flower Withers   by Dennis C Mariotis

good days and bad days. Don't call anything off! We both know I'm only gonna get worse! There won't be any *'feeling better'* in the future." Russ hugged her before turning to exit the kitchen. They talked and laughed as Rose walked with him through her living room up to the front door. Opening the door Russ turned to her and hugged her tightly before turning and walking out the door. Rose stood at the front doorway and watched Russ as he walked to his car, enter it, and leave before closing the door and going to her bedroom for a much needed nap. She laid her head on her pillow and thought about all the things on her bucket list before falling into a deep sleep that lasted about three hours.

       The next morning Russ picked up an anxious Rose and headed off to Fort Benning, Georgia. Rose read the additional information included with the letter from the army regarding the protocols and expectations of this event. Two and a half hours, and almost one hundred thirty miles later they arrived at the front gates of Fort

Before The Flower Withers   by Dennis C Mariotis

Benning. Stopping their car, it took another fifteen minutes for the military to inspect the car and all their paperwork before allowing them to enter. Meeting them at the front gate was an army officer Captain Johnson, who was in charge of civilian relations.

Addressing Rose and Russ, the Captain had them enter a military vehicle and drove them to the training area. There they exited the vehicle and entered a building where they waited for the soldier who was appointed and in charge of Rose's tank ride experience. Rose was too excited to sit down while they waited. Instead she stood by a window and watched the soldiers in the field going through their drills. She smiled as she watched them marching, running, and chuckled when she watched a Drill Sergeant yelling at a new frightened recruit while the Sergeant stood nose to nose with him.

The distant sound of an armored vehicle drew her attention. She

***Before The Flower Withers**   by Dennis C Mariotis*

looked around but could not see which direction it was coming from. As the sound grew more intense it finally came into view as Rose's eyes opened wider. Then her jaw dropped as the thunderous sound of the tank arrived and stopped in front of the window. Hearing this, Russ stood up and joined her. The tank's noise suddenly quieted. They watched it sitting still. Within a minute the top hatch opened and a soldier climbed out of the tank and made his way down to ground level.

       The office door opened and in walked the soldier who climbed out of the tank. Standing at the front of an officer's desk the soldier saluted the officer and handing him an envelope he said, "Corporal Baker reporting sir." Returning the salute the officer took the envelope from the corporal. Before opening it the officer replied, "At ease Corporal." Opening the envelope the officer looked at Rose and motioned her to come to the desk. Walking to him she stopped. The officer said, "Miss Miles. Corporal Baker is assigned to give you a tour and ride in

Before The Flower Withers   by Dennis C Mariotis

a tank." Turning to the soldier the officer said, "Corporal Baker? You will escort and assist Miss Miles into the tank. There you will drive Miss Miles around the designated area and return her here in fifteen minutes. That's all."

The soldier saluted the officer as he replied, "Yes sir!" He then turned and escorted Rose out the door and to a ramp where she stood and waited for the soldier to drive the tank to her. The ramp was high enough to allow people access to large military vehicles in the event they needed aid. Russ watched all the action from the safety of the office. The roaring noise of the tank as it approached Rose made her smile as she anticipated being physically able to perform another item on her bucket list. With a lot of help from several soldiers, Rose was inside the tank along with Corporal Baker.

The Corporal drove the tank slowly away from the ramp. It took about thirty seconds in low gear to

Before The Flower Withers   by Dennis C Mariotis

clear the area. After that the tank sped up. Rose was having a wonderful time being in something that big, powerful, and dangerous. She listened to the soldier describe how tanks are used in a real war and that this one saw a lot of action in Iraq. She watched him use the steering mechanisms very carefully for about ten minutes. She asked, "Corporal Baker? Do you mind if I drive for a minute?" He looked around and seeing a great deal of clearance he stopped the tank and said, "I guess you can't do any harm in this spot. But only for one minute, and only if you promise not to mention anything about me letting you drive, or I'll get in a lot of trouble." She smiled and crossed her chest with her finger, "Cross my heart and hope to die...I promise I won't say a thing!"

    Switching positions, Rose was now in the driver's seat. For the next minute she drove the tank like a pro. She was having a great time going up a hill, then down another hill. She moved backwards and forwards with instruction from the Corporal who

Before The Flower Withers   by Dennis C Mariotis

allowed her to drive it for another minute. When he directed her to stop, she did so. They switched seats but before continuing the drive, the soldier demonstrated the operation of the tank's turret. This is the long cannon like weapon on the tank. Rose watched from a window in the tank as he maneuvered the long turret. Fascinated by it Rose asked, "Do you mind if I try it?" The Corporal answered as he let her have the controls, "Not at all, here you go." Rose smiled and said, "Thanks!" as she took over and operated the turret. Up and down, side to side, Rose was having a better time than she ever imagined. While operating the turret Rose asked, "Do you mind if I pushed some of these buttons and play with some of the other controls like the trigger?" Corporal Baker answered, "Not at all. It's a dead tank. You can't do any harm."

Meanwhile back at the office, Russ smiled watching the tank drive around the designated area. Diverting his attention was a Humvee that streaked across the yard headed

Before The Flower Withers   by Dennis C Mariotis

toward the office. It was kicking up dust in every direction. Coming to a screeching halt it raised a cloud of dust. A soldier came running out of it and headed to the office. Opening the door the soldier ran directly to the desk and stood in front of the officer. Saluting him with a very serious expression he began speaking very fast, "I have some VERY serious news sir!" The officer wasted no time, "What is it soldier?" The soldier swallowed hard and said, "Major Wilson radioed me to come here and stop the current tank demonstration immediately." The officer's expression quickly turned into a seriously concerned look as he stood and asked, "Why?" The soldier responded, "Unknown to Corporal Baker, the tank assigned to him was the wrong tank. *Instead of a dead tank, he was given a live tank!*" The officer cringed and clenching his teeth with anger and disbelief he raised his voice, **"That's a live tank?"**

With a great deal of concern Russ ran to the officer and asked, "What's a live tank?" Picking up

Before The Flower Withers   by Dennis C Mariotis

his radio to call Corporal Baker, the officer told the soldier, "You explain. I'm gonna try to reach Baker!" The soldier turned to Russ and explained, "A live tank is a tank that is ready for full combat operation. There's live ammunition in it and it's loaded and ready to launch 125 millimeter artillery shells!" Russ' expression turned to all out fear. With a frightened look Russ said, "Hurry up and stop it. You don't know my grandmother. She's a very curious person!"

Inside the tank Corporal Baker received a radio message. Picking his radio up he pushed down the button and answered it, "Corporal Baker here, go ahead!" At the same time Rose was playing with the turret's controls as she imagined she was on a real live battle field. Hearing the message, Corporal Baker screamed at Rose who was aiming the turret while her finger was on the trigger, *"It's live...Let it go! Stop! Don't touch that trigger!"*

Before The Flower Withers   by Dennis C Mariotis

Corporal Baker's sudden screaming startled Rose so much that it turned an otherwise calm cool drive into a deadly one. Startling her made her tighten up and pull the trigger. The blast sent her back in her seat as the fire from the launched artillery shell shot out of the front of the turret. Recovering from the tank's rocking back from firing the shell, Rose rubbed her head and asked, "What the hell was that?" With a look of shock and surprise, Corporal Baker answered, *"That was a live round you fired by pulling the trigger!"* Rose was surprised and momentarily in shock. Regaining her composure quickly, with fear and nervousness she asked, "Did I hit anything?"

The artillery shell she fired whistled through the air and headed towards one of the army barracks containing eighty five soldiers who were relaxing in the building after a day of heavy drilling. Inside the barrack the Sergeant on duty looked up when he heard the familiar whistling sound of the artillery shell getting

Before The Flower Withers   by Dennis C Mariotis

closer. With a look of fear he quickly jumped to his feet and yelled, "Incoming!" as loud as he could. Hearing him, as well as the whistling from the artillery shell screaming closer, all the soldiers immediately fell to the floor and braced themselves for the blast.

The whistling shell landed and exploded. The eighty foot ball of smoke and fire, and the sound from the explosion was seen and heard from the entire base when it struck and destroyed a large metal dumpster standing outside and very close to the barracks. Soldiers from all over the base ran to the tank with their rifles in their hands, ready for combat.

Confronting the tank, the soldiers waited with their rifles pointed at the tank's hatch. When the hatch was pushed open, Rose very slowly emerged. Looking around at all the angry expressions on the faces of the soldiers who she almost blew up, Rose was petrified at the sight of all those rifles pointed at her. With a surprised

Before The Flower Withers   by Dennis C Mariotis

expression on her face she slowly put her hands on top of her head and said, "Don't shoot...I give up!" When the soldiers saw it was an old woman, they were relieved as they drew back their weapons and stood down. With her hands on her head, Rose looked down into the tank at Corporal Baker. Nodding her head she said, "I believe the demonstration is over." With sweat pouring from his brow, Corporal Baker looked up at her and breathing very heavily he nodded in agreement.

After several soldiers helped her out of the tank and down to the ground, Rose met up with Russ who was waiting for her inside the Humvee he rode in with the officer. She quietly entered the vehicle, then the officer drove them away. They were escorted by a team of soldiers who glared at them until they left the base.

During the two and a half hour drive back home they didn't speak very much from the shock of the situation. Breaking the silence, Russ

Before The Flower Withers   *by Dennis C Mariotis*

turned to Rose and asked, "You're pretty quiet grandma. Are you all right?" Expressionless, Rose stared straight ahead through the car's windshield and shook her head as she replied in a serious tone, "Uh uh! I almost killed some brave American soldiers!"

Trying to help her out of her distress by changing the subject, Russ asked, "What do you want to do next?" Snapping out of her shock she answered, "Those guys are pretty upset with me. I think we better leave the country for awhile!" Russ smirked and nodded as he continued driving.

Before The Flower Withers   *by Dennis C Mariotis*

CHAPTER 8
A Short Trip To Paris

On their way home from Fort Benning, they decided to pick up some Chinese food for dinner. Arriving at her home later that day Russ and Rose sat at her dining room table eating and discussing the next event from her bucket list. Rose was insistent with her need to get away from Georgia after the tank incident.

Before The Flower Withers   by Dennis C Mariotis

Looking through the list she put her fork down and picked up a piece of paper.

She concentrated on the list as she perused each unchecked item with her index finger until she stopped on the one that interested her most. Smiling she showed the paper to Russ for him to see her selection. He looked at it and thought a moment. He smiled and looked at Rose who was nodding. He nodded back and said, "That's great. I was hoping you would choose that one. I always wanted to see the Eifel Tower. Let's do it!"

Rose was so excited that she put the paper down, stood up, and quickly ran to her telephone. After getting the phone number for Air France she called them for reservations. With her credit card in hand Rose spoke to the Sales Representative and made all the arrangements.

Hanging up the phone Rose went back to the dining room table and sat down. Smiling at Russ she explained their itinerary, "We're all

Before The Flower Withers   by Dennis C Mariotis

set for next weekend. It's a one night stay. We leave on Thursday and arrive Friday morning. We'll have lunch on the West Bank, then go sightseeing the rest of the day. We fly out on Saturday and arrive home on Sunday!" Russ nodded and smiled as he commented, "That's so exciting. I can't wait!" Thinking about Rose's condition concerned him. With a serious expression he continued, "You looked really tired on our way home today. I hope you're not wearing yourself out with all this excitement!" Rose shook her head and looking at him she snickered, "I'll make sure I get plenty of rest." She laughed and pointing her finger in his face she joked, "And you just try to keep up with me!" Laughing before getting back to his meal he replied, "I'll do my best!" They resumed eating their dinner as they laughed and joked about their upcoming trip.

The week seemed to pass very slowly for both of them since they were counting the minutes before their trip. When Thursday finally came they drove to the Atlanta airport where Russ

Before The Flower Withers   by Dennis C Mariotis

parked the car and escorted Rose to the terminal. Since they only took one carryon bag each they were able to quickly check in and get through security. Rose like Russ, was very excited about this trip and she showed no signs of fatigue whatsoever. She even outpaced Russ on her way to the Air France gate where their plane waited. They sat for about an hour until it was time to board the plane. About a half hour after boarding the plane taxied down the runway and took off. The non-stop flight took about nine hours.

Landing in Paris they exited the plane and the airport and went straight to a taxi stand where they boarded a taxi that took them to their hotel. After checking into their hotel they decided to freshen up before meeting in the lobby. At about twelve noon they left the hotel on their way to lunch on the West Bank. At Rose's request the cab driver drove slow to allow her to look at all the restaurants before making her

Before The Flower Withers   by Dennis C Mariotis

selection. She looked out the window but could not decide.

Russ snickered every time at Rose's comical attempt at pronouncing some common French words. She asked the driver, "Pardonemwear Monsewer, but can you suggest a good place to have lunch?" The driver snickered as he pulled the cab over in front of a restaurant. After stopping and pointing out the window, he turned to Rose and with a heavy French accent he answered, "Madame? I suggest 'zat one. It's very gude!"

Rose stared at the restaurant for a moment. Russ and the driver laughed out loud when Rose tried to pronounce the name, *"La Creepery?"* Correcting her, the driver replied, "Not *Creepery. La Cre-pe-rie!* They serve excellent authentic French cuisine!" Russ encouraged Rose as she was trying to make up her mind. "Grandma, it looks like a fine place to me." Rose nodded and replied, *"Okay. La Creepery it is!"* Rose turned to the cab driver and said, "Mercy bucket!"

Before The Flower Withers   by Dennis C Mariotis

Acknowledging her with a nod and a smile, the cab driver gave up trying to correct her. Russ exited the cab and waited for Rose to get out after she paid the driver. Walking up to an outside table they sat down and had lunch. For about an hour they talked and thoroughly enjoyed their meal along with a couple of glasses of wine. The waiter was friendly and very accommodating.

After finishing their lunch they decided to stroll around the area and enjoy the beautiful day and the incredible sights. An hour later Russ hailed a taxi cab. It was a short drive to the Eifel Tower. Upon arriving, they exited the cab and stopped for a moment as they gazed upon the Tower. They were awestruck by its magnificence. Looking up with her hand shielding the sun from her eyes Rose said, "Wow! It's beautiful. Seeing it in person is so much better than all those pictures." Russ nodded as he stared at the Tower and replied, "Yes it is! Well? What do you say we get our tickets and see what it looks like from

Before The Flower Withers   *by Dennis C Mariotis*

the top?" Rose smiled and hooked his arm as they started walking to the Tower entrance.

Stopping first at a street vendor selling ice cream they decided to each get a large ice cream cone. Rose chose French Vanilla and Russ chose Chocolate. Walking to the Tower entrance Rose bought two tickets at the booth. Entering the base area they walked up the steps. The first area they stopped was about twenty feet up. Walking to the railing to let others by Rose needed to catch her breath. "Are you all right grandma?" Russ asked with concern in his voice as he watched her huff and puff. Leaning up against the rail Rose nodded and replied, "Yeah! It's just one of the things Dr. Bill told me. He said to expect shortness of breath from doing simple things. Gimme a minute to catch my breath."

Russ stood next to her against the rail. Rose turned and looking down she noticed a couple standing directly below her. They were

Before The Flower Withers   *by Dennis C Mariotis*

taking pictures of each other. Rose looked at Russ and chuckled when she noticed that the woman was about a foot taller than her husband. He was a short bald man who made awkward looking poses while his wife took his picture. Rose stared at him with curiosity as he made a very unusual pose and waited for his wife to take his picture. Leaning over to get a better look she strained so much that she accidentally dropped her French Vanilla cone. Rose let out a gasp, "Oh no!" as the cone made a beeline for the man.

It was perfect timing. Just as the man's wife took his picture the ice cream cone landed a bulls-eye on top of his head. The crowd around the area where the couple was taking pictures saw the incident. Roaring laughter and snide comments came from people in the crowd. His wife let out a loud laugh when she saw it and again when she looked at the picture she took. But the man was not happy. He looked around and became angrier from his embarrassment. Looking up he saw Rose waving at him. When the crowd

Before The Flower Withers   by Dennis C Mariotis

quieted down Rose called to him, "Hey Monserwer! I'm terribly sorry. It was an accident."

The man was not in the mood for apologies. He waved his fist at Rose and said in a heavy French accent, "What's wrong with you Madame, you clumsy idiot!" Hearing this Rose tried to sympathize with him but was somewhat upset by the man's anger. Then she offered her apologies again as she cupped her hands around her mouth and yelled down to him, "I said I was sorry. What else do you want me to do?" The man looked up and with a hateful and disgusted expression he yelled where everyone could hear him, "You can be more careful you stupid American!" This angered Rose as she glared at him for his nastiness. She stood at the railing and watched as his wife helped him clean the ice cream off his head so they could take another picture.

His comment really irritated Rose to the point where she wanted to walk down the stairs and smack him across his mouth. Watching as

Before The Flower Withers   by Dennis C Mariotis

the man went back to his pose; he waited patiently as his wife picked up her camera and took her time getting it ready before pointing it at him. Turning quickly to Russ, Rose took the ice cream cone out of his hand and said, "I'll get you another one!" Knowing his grandmother's temper Russ knew right away what she had in mind. He chuckled as he watched her in action. She snickered and said to Russ, "Add this to my bucket list!" Then she turned and holding the ice cream cone over the rail she looked down with one eye closed and took aim. Dropping the cone on her target below she once again made a bulls-eye as it splat-landed on top of the man's head just as his wife took his picture.

      Once again the crowd around the man saw the incident and now the laughter was even more intense. They hushed pretty quickly in anticipation of the verbal exchange as they saw him turn and look up at Rose who was smiling and waving at him. The man again, waved his fist at Rose and yelled, *"Sacre bleu! Stupid American!*

Before The Flower Withers   by Dennis C Mariotis

Why did you do that?" The crowd erupted after they heard Rose's response as she waved her fist at him and yelled back, "Because you look better with chocolate, Frenchie!"

Rose and Russ left the area and continued their tour of the Eifel Tower. They laughed and joked about the ice cream incident. They enjoyed the view from the top and stayed there long enough to see the awesome sight of the Tower and Paris lit up after dusk. When it came time to leave, reality hit as Russ had to assist Rose more than usual when they came down the Tower and went back to the hotel. He could tell that her condition was worsening. He helped her up and into her hotel room and into bed. Locking the door after he exited her room he quietly walked to his room. Entering his room he walked to the window where he took a deep breath and sighed as he looked out over the beautiful Paris skyline.

The next morning Russ helped Rose as they checked out of the

Before The Flower Withers   by Dennis C Mariotis

hotel and headed for the airport. Arm in arm while they walked Rose had to stop several times to catch her breath. Rose recovered somewhat after the cab ride to the airport. Rose tried to alleviate Russ' concern by explaining what she was going through. Boarding the plane she sat in her seat and took a dose of the painkiller medicine prescribed by Dr. Bill. With a pillow under her head and a blanket draped across her body she fell into a deep sleep for almost half of the trip back home.

CHAPTER 9
Las Vegas-Here Comes Rose!

It was about two weeks later when Rose felt well enough to move forward with her bucket list. During her two-week respite Rose spent time locally with her family and friends. She also visited her attorney to ensure her Will reflected her wishes. She did not want to leave anything undone. Feeling confident that

Before The Flower Withers   by Dennis C Mariotis

she had all her final affairs in order, Rose called Russ and told him she was ready to finish the remainder of her bucket list. Wanting to get them done within the next month she forced herself to put aside all her feelings of anxiety and stress.

The next evening Russ drove to Rose's house to have dinner and discuss the best way to arrange the completion of the remaining items. She prepared Russ' favorite meal, Chicken Cacciatore over Rice Pilaf. Sitting down to eat Russ' mouth watered when he smelled the aroma of the meal she prepared. Bringing it into the dining room she sat it down on the table. Then she poured a couple of glasses of fine wine before sitting down and joining him for dinner.

As they were serving themselves the food Russ admired the dinnerware. He smiled at her and said, "These plates and glasses are really elegant. I never ate off of them before." Rose snickered as she looked at him and replied, "Neither has anyone

Before The Flower Withers   by Dennis C Mariotis

else. I've had these for over forty years and this is the first time I ever used them!" Russ shook his head and with a confused expression he asked, "Why not?" Rose nodded and replied, "Because they were so expensive and I didn't want to break any of them and ruin the set. So for forty years they sat on display in my China Cabinet." He thought for a few seconds then asked, "But why didn't you use them for special occasions?" Rose stopped and stared at him. She sighed and shook her head as she answered, "I was waiting for a very special occasion. I just didn't realize until my last doctor visit that every day was a special occasion." Understanding exactly what she meant, Russ nodded.

Keeping with their agenda after they finished dinner, they moved to the kitchen where they sat at the table. Looking over the remaining items on Rose's Bucket List they came up with an arrangement they felt could best accomplish all of them within a month. They planned to travel to Las Vegas, Nevada first. Rose listened

Before The Flower Withers   by Dennis C Mariotis

carefully as Russ explained, "Grandma. I did my research and came up with this plan: We fly to Las Vegas first. There we can accomplish five of the last eight items on your list. Obviously you can gamble. That's one. They have some great breathtaking high-risk rides. That's two. There's a circus in town for the next couple of months that offers all kinds of rides on exotic horses, giraffes, and elephants. That's three. They have a park that offers all kinds of rides including motorcycle rides. That's four. And last they have about a thousand well known tattoo parlors owned by famous tattoo artists. How does that sound so far?"

Rose scratched her head and thought for a moment while she looked over the list and considered Russ' action plan. Clearing her throat she nodded answering, "Looks like you did your homework. That works for me. How long do you think we should plan to stay?" Russ looked at Rose and immediately answered, "That all depends on how you're feeling. If you get tired like you did in Paris it could take us

Before The Flower Withers   by Dennis C Mariotis

about two weeks. If you're well it'll take about one week." Rose nodded, "You're right. Let's plan on two weeks. If we complete it in one week, we can rest and relax and enjoy the second week. Great! Now what about the remaining three items?"

Russ scratched his head and looked at Rose. Shaking his head he answered, "There are only two remaining items that you'll be taking an active part. The third one is cremation." Rose chuckled, "You're wrong about my active part in my cremation. That's the only one that I get to do all by myself!" Russ' smile didn't last long thinking about that one. He replied, "You're right. With the exception of the last item the other two pose problems. As for climbing a mountain, you're growing weaker and that's gonna take a lot of strength and stamina on your part." Rose leaned back and thought about that one. She looked at Russ and replied, "We'll look into that when we get back from Vegas. What about the last one?"

Before The Flower Withers   by Dennis C Mariotis

Russ shrugged his shoulders as he struggled with that item. Shaking his head he looked at Rose and said, "Changing someone's world! That one's got me baffled. Do you have any thoughts about how you can impact someone's life that you change their entire world?" Rose nodded and said, "I have a few ideas that I'm considering. I'll let you know as soon as I've made up my mind." Russ nodded and said, "That sounds great! Now when do you want to go to Vegas?"

Rose reached for a manila envelope at the end of the kitchen table. Opening it she handed Russ a package containing airplane tickets and hotel reservations. Russ looked over the packet and smiling he said, "The reservations are for the day after tomorrow for two weeks in Vegas." Placing them back into the envelope he turned to Rose, "Grandma. You're something else! You came up with the same time I did! How did you know what I was planning?" Reaching across the table she put her hand over his and chuckled saying, "Great minds think

Before The Flower Withers   by Dennis C Mariotis

alike!" She smiled and continued, "Just remember, while we're in Vegas, call me Rose, not grandma." He smiled and nodded, "You got it Rose. Just practicing!"

Two days later Russ and Rose flew from Atlanta to Las Vegas. When they landed they took a taxi to the hotel where they checked in separate rooms. Rose made sure her room had an access door between hers and Russ'. They spent their first night driving around the town sightseeing. Finding a nice restaurant to have dinner was easy. During their dinner Rose shared stories about her life. She told Russ things he never knew happened to her and her family. Most of the stories were comical. Russ gained a better appreciation for Rose and his grandpa as well as his parents. After dinner they went back to their hotel where they walked around the casino and all the other hotel amenities like the swimming pool and the auditorium which staged special events. They were very impressed to see how much hotels in Vegas offered within one building.

Before The Flower Withers   by Dennis C Mariotis

When their tour of the hotel finished it was getting late and Rose was tired. They were sitting at a table in the hotel's lounge having a cocktail when Rose reached into her purse and took out her medicine. Seeing this concerned Russ and he asked, "Are you okay grandma, I mean Rose?" Letting out a short moan she answered, "I'm not gonna try to pretend nothing is wrong. Just to let you know, the pain has been coming on stronger at times." Russ' grew more concerned and his expression showed it. He pointed to the strong pain medication in her hand and said, "They put horses to sleep with that stuff you're taking! Are you sure you should be chasing those meds down with a Harvey Wallbanger?"

She smiled as she put the pill in her mouth and took a big gulp from her cocktail. After swallowing her medicine she looked at Russ and chuckled saying, "What's it gonna do, kill me?" Russ shook his head, grinned, and then replied, "Well I'd like to keep you around a little bit longer." Rose grimaced a little and

Before The Flower Withers   by Dennis C Mariotis

said, "Don't worry. I'll be all right. There's one good thing about this drink, it sure makes the medicine work better." They both laughed at her comical remark. It took about ten minutes for the effects of the mixture of alcohol and pain medication to kick in, and Rose actually felt better.

Standing up first, Russ helped Rose to her feet. She winked at him and said, "I need to lie down before I fall down and go to sleep on the lounge floor." As he hooked her arm with his Russ replied, "I gotcha Rose." Turning they headed in the direction of the elevator which took them up to their rooms. Opening the door Rose turned to Russ, hugged him, and kissed his cheek. She entered her room walking in under her own power. Russ watched as she slowly walked to her bed and laid down. He knew her routine when she was very tired. She would fall asleep for about three hours, and then wake up, change her clothes, and go back to sleep. Russ made sure there was a light left on so that she knew where she was when she woke up. Closing and securing

Before The Flower Withers   by Dennis C Mariotis

her door, Russ walked to his room. He was not going to go off on his own. He was very mindful knowing this was Rose's time and he wanted to be well rested for her sake. Entering his room, he showered and changed clothes, and then laid down on the bed, and watched television until he fell asleep.

Before The Flower Withers   by Dennis C Mariotis

CHAPTER 10
Rose Tries Her Luck

After an early breakfast Rose and Russ took a sightseeing tour bus ride. They marveled at all the architectural grandeur of the beautiful hotel buildings. Each one was built with a unique theme. After their bus tour they went back to their hotel where they enjoyed a small lunch and an afternoon of relaxation. Rose took in a massage at the hotel's health spa while Russ

Before The Flower Withers   by Dennis C Mariotis

went for a swim and to check out the women in the hotel's pool. After her massage Rose walked back to her room for a nap while Russ relaxed in a lounge chair by the pool as he conversed with some of the hotel's female guests that he befriended.

Checking on the time he realized it was getting late. Excusing himself Russ left the pool area and headed to his room where he showered and changed for dinner. He stayed in his room patiently waiting for Rose to call for him when she was ready. It was almost six thirty when she knocked on the door which connected their rooms. Opening the door he smiled when he saw Rose in a stunning gown.

Nodding he smiled as he looked Rose up and down, "Rose, you look beautiful!" She winked and smiled, "Thank you honey. I feel terrific too. That massage and nap rejuvenated me. I didn't need any of that nasty medicine, but I did have a Harvey Wallbanger after I woke up. The bar here makes it with fresh squeezed orange juice. What

Before The Flower Withers   by Dennis C Mariotis

a huge difference!" Russ chuckled, "I'm glad you're feeling great! But I'm gonna warn you! You better not drink while you're gambling because that's how people lose a lot of money!" Rose shook her head, "Oh don't worry about that. They charge a lot for drinks at this place. I don't wanna run up a huge tab our first day here." Russ chuckled saying, "You won't while you're playing because at the casino players are given free drinks of their choice!" Rose nodded and snickered, "Well then I'll rely on you to keep an eye on me!" They both laughed heartily at Russ' reply, "Just drink responsibly Rose! I don't wanna see you lose your money, and your bra tonight!"

Exiting through Rose's room they took the elevator to the dining level. There they had their choice of different cuisines. Looking around Russ asked, "Well Rose, what do you feel like eating? Italian, Steak, Seafood, Chinese, Japanese Sushi, American, or Mexican?" Rose looked around then asked him, "I don't know. What are you in the mood for?" Russ

Before The Flower Withers   by Dennis C Mariotis

looked around again and answered, "I'm leaning toward the Sushi Bar." Rose snickered and answered, "I like my sushi well done! How about the seafood place? They offer us a choice there, raw or cooked." Russ chuckled, "Seafood it is!" as he extended his arm and escorted Rose to the restaurant.

After dinner and dessert they stayed a little while and talked until about eight o'clock. Leaving the restaurant they took the elevator to the casino level. Exiting the elevator they were greeted with the flashing lights and exciting sounds of the casino. Rose looked around and smiled when she saw the propaganda all around the slot machine area which they used to tempt and suck in unsuspecting people. The displays were of massive jackpots, great prizes, and pictures of smiling people having a great time as they stared at the huge payouts from the machines.

Russ looked around and then watched Rose who was grinning at the sights and sounds. Talking loud

Before The Flower Withers   by Dennis C Mariotis

over all the noise he asked, "See anything you want to try?" She spoke loudly back answering, "Nothing's changed in thirty years since your grandpa showed me a casino. The only thing different is the computerization of these one-armed-bandits." Russ asked, "What's a one-armed-bandit?" Rose snickered and answered, "That's my generation's term for a slot machine. Back then they had one handle that you pulled after you put coins into them. These are more sophisticated. No coins or handles. It's all buttons and player cards! Same ol' crap...different generation!"

They walked and looked around some more until Russ asked, "Well Rose? Anything interest you yet?" She nodded and pointed to a table, "Yes. Craps. That looks like fun!" Walking to the Craps table with Rose, Russ asked, "Do you know how to play?" Rose shrugged her shoulders and said, "Your grandpa showed me how to play at home many years ago but I forgot a lot. I didn't know what I was doing when we played. All I know is that I beat him!

Before The Flower Withers   by Dennis C Mariotis

But I think he let me beat him." Arriving and standing at the table watching the action, Russ snickered and replied, "There's a big difference here...These guys aren't nice like grandpa."

Rose smiled as she took two hundred dollars out of her purse and exchanged it for chips. Seeing this Russ asked, "Aren't you gonna wait and see how the game is played?" Rose looked around before she answered, "Sure I am. Having this stack of chips here makes me a Player. I'm not gonna bet anything. All I want is a Harvey Wallbanger!" Russ laughed as the waitress came up to Rose and took her drink order. Rose turned and winked at Russ.

After a couple of drinks Rose was beginning to feel the effects of the liquid courage. Then it came time to switch players who rolled the dice. A man gave his turn to Rose when he said to the worker controlling the game, "She looks like a lucky lady." Turning to Rose the man asked, "What's

Before The Flower Withers   by Dennis C Mariotis

your name lovely lady?" She answered, "Rose!" Turning to the casino worker he said, "Give Rose my turn!" At first she refused but the man along with the other players encouraged her until she broke down and accepted.

The casino worker pushed the dice to Rose and said, "New shooter. Place your bets everyone!" Rose placed a bet of fifty dollars and waited for everyone to place their bets before she was allowed to touch the dice. Once cleared, she picked up the dice and shook them in her hand imitating the way she saw the shooter before her did it. The others at the table cheered her on, "Come on Lucky Rose! Roll a seven!" Rose tossed the dice and they cheered when the dice stopped on a six and a one. The worker shouted, "Seven. A winner." Paying out their bets she waited until the others placed their bets.

The worker asked her if she wanted to Press her bet. She didn't understand until they explained that since she won she could let her bet and

Before The Flower Withers   by Dennis C Mariotis

winnings ride or continue or double her bet. She looked around and laughed saying, "Sure. Press my bet. Let it ride partner! Yahoo!" Rolling the dice again the casino worker shouted, "Seven a winner!" Rose continued on a streak that lasted for over half an hour. Several times the Pit Boss came to the table and examined the dice before allowing her to continue rolling them. She was laughing and clapping along with the others at the table. One man looked at her and said, *"Come on baby! One more time!"* Rolling the dice the casino worker said, "Seven...a winner!" The man jumped up and down along with his friends. He pointed at Rose and said, *"Yeah! Thank you Rose baby! That Monster Roll just made me fifteen thousand!"*

Before Rose was given the dice for her next roll Russ looked at her and said, "You haven't touched your money on the table." With all the excitement, Rose didn't realize that she let her bet continue to build with every roll. Looking at the table she asked Russ, "Which stack is mine?" Russ

Before The Flower Withers   by Dennis C Mariotis

laughed when he pointed to the huge stack of chips ranging from ten dollar chips to one thousand dollar chips. Rose's eyes lit up with surprise as she looked at Russ and asked, "What do I do now?" Russ advised her, "Rose. You've won well over twenty thousand dollars. I suggest you pick up everything except for your initial bet of fifty dollars!" Rose shook her head and asked, "But why when I'm doing so good?" Russ answered, "Because every gambler's good luck, no matter how good, eventually turns bad. *One bad roll and you've lost it all!*"

Her eyes grew wide open with a surprised expression as she said, *"Holy crap! Fifty bucks is one thing but twenty thousand? Now way!"* That was enough to convince her to remove all but fifty dollars from her bet. It took about five more rolls before her streak came to an end. Everyone at the table congratulated her on a great run. They all made out with huge winnings. The casino worker congratulated Rose, then he turned to the Pit Boss and with a sigh of relief said, "I'm glad that old lady crapped

Before The Flower Withers   by Dennis C Mariotis

out! I was afraid she was gonna wind up owning the place!"

Russ helped Rose gather her chips and walked with her over to the cashier where he stood about fifteen feet away after he signed some paperwork along with Rose. Then she cashed in all her chips. She shook her head and snickered when the cashier gave her five thousand in cash and a check for over nineteen thousand dollars. Without his knowledge she had the cashier make out the check to her and Russ. Putting the check in her purse she left the cashier and met up with Russ. Looking around he asked, "Do you want to continue or are you too tired?" Rose smiled and said, "I'm just beginning to have fun. Let's have another drink and go visit that Roulette table. I'm still feeling lucky." Russ smiled and said, "I'm glad you're having fun and winning." Rose shook her head and said, "I'm glad you told me about my winnings or I would've lost all of it."

Before The Flower Withers   by Dennis C Mariotis

Walking over to the no-limit Roulette table with a drink in their hands they sat down and watched for about ten minutes. Rose then decided to play. Taking out a roll of hundreds Rose counted out her money and gave it to the Roulette worker who counted it out on the table and called to the Pit Boss for approval, "Cashing five thousand!" Russ was surprised as he looked at Rose and said, "Five grand?" She looked at him and chuckled, "Why not? I can't take it with me!" Counting out the chips the worker pushed them in front of Rose.

Rose waited for a couple of spins of the wheel before she decided to gamble. At first she was very cautious and played very conservatively. She bet ten or twenty dollars and only won a few times. It took about an hour for her to lose almost a thousand dollars. She looked at Russ and said, "This game is terrible! I tried playing all my lucky numbers but that obviously didn't work!" Russ shook his head and replied,

Before The Flower Withers   *by Dennis C Mariotis*

"At least you left with a bundle from the Craps table."

Rose was becoming frustrated from the lack of excitement at the Roulette game. She looked at Russ and said, "I'm getting tired." Russ looked at her to be sure she wasn't pushing herself too far. Then he questioned her, "Do you want to go back to your room and rest?" She answered, "Yeah, but first I wanna make my last bet. What's your lucky number honey?" He answered, "I've got a couple of lucky numbers. 5 and 33. Take your pick."

Rose thought for a moment, then she took half of her chips and handed them to him as she said, "Here, take this two thousand dollars in chips. The other two thousand I'm betting on number 28. That's your birth date." Pushing all two thousand dollars in chips on 28 Rose looked at him, winked, and nodded. The Roulette worker called to alert his Pit Boss, "Two thousand bet Straight Up on 28!" He waited for his supervisor who walked up

Before The Flower Withers   by Dennis C Mariotis

next to him and looked at the bet before giving the go ahead. Hearing this drew a crowd of curious onlookers who slowly gathered around the table waiting for the worker to spin the wheel and set the little white ball into play. Russ and Rose looked around and smiled at everyone. Russ stood up and said to everyone, "This is my good friend Rose. Let's all cheer for her!"

The Pit Boss nodded to the Roulette worker who spun the wheel and waited momentarily before releasing the ball. People from the crowd shouted words of encouragement and cheered her. She sat there with a huge smile. Rose let out a loud laugh and continued to laugh hysterically after Russ leaned over and whispered in her ear, "You had four Harvey Wallbangers. IF you win, whatever you do...don't jump on the Roulette table and recite any of those nasty limericks at the cheering crowd!"

With the wheel still spinning the Roulette worker released the ball. After watching the white ball go round and round a couple of times

Before The Flower Withers   by Dennis C Mariotis

Rose looked up and tightly closed her eyes. When she heard the ball drop and make the clacking ricochet sounds as it bounced around the wheel, she clenched her teeth and held up her hands with her fingers crossed. The crowd made Ooo and Aaah sounds as the ball looked like it was going to stop as it bounced around in and out of the other losing number slots. Then when the ball stopped the crowd didn't see the slot where it finally came to rest until one person shouted, *"28!!! You won!"*

The crowd let out a thunderous roar of cheering and screaming. Not believing it at first Rose opened her eyes and leaned over to see for herself. Looking down at the wheel slowly spinning she saw the little white ball sitting comfortably in the number 28 slot. Looking up at the computerized board was the number 28 flashing. As Russ hugged her and congratulated her she looked at the Roulette worker who was smiling. Then she looked at the Pit Boss who was staring at her with a look of

Before The Flower Withers   by Dennis C Mariotis

disbelief. She smiled and winked at him just before he turned and left.

They waited at the table where she handed Russ the two thousand in chips that she used to bet on number 28 and asked, "Well that was really exciting. How much did I win? Ten thousand or was it more?" Russ laughed and answered, "You mean you don't know how much this game pays out?" She shrugged her shoulders and shook her head, "No I don't." Russ got the attention of the worker who asked her to wait while they worked on getting her an official casino marker to take to the cashier and asked him, "Excuse me but would you please tell her how much she won?" The worker smiled and answered, "With your two thousand dollar bet, at a thirty five to one payout, you won seventy thousand dollars!" Rose was startled by that amount that she sat there with a look of shock and disbelief.

It took the Pit Boss about five minutes to return to the table. Handing her the marker he said,

Before The Flower Withers   by Dennis C Mariotis

"I was in the same amount of shock that you were in when that ball landed on 28. I never saw anyone win that much money before. Congratulations! Take this to the cashier window to claim your winnings." Rose stood and thanked him, and then took Russ by the arm and walked to the cashier window where she handed her the marker. Once again Russ completed some paperwork along with Rose at the cashier window. Then he walked away and stood about ten feet from her and watched the action in the casino as Rose cashed in her remaining chips and collected her Roulette winnings. She had the cashier pay her out with five thousand dollars in cash and the remaining sixty nine thousand dollars in a check made out to her and Russ.

       Meeting up with Russ after cashing out her position Rose and Russ decided to call it a night since it was almost twelve o'clock. Walking to the far end of the casino they took the elevator up to their floor. Exiting the elevator, Russ walked Rose to her room and waited for her to be safely

Before The Flower Withers   by Dennis C Mariotis

inside. Then he closed and secured her room door before going to his room. Inside Rose's room she changed her clothes. Before laying down to sleep she reached into her purse. Smiling she pulled out the two checks and looked at them before folding them and putting them into the hotel safe.

Walking into her bathroom Rose stopped as she felt a sudden deep and sharp sensation throughout her body. She grimaced as she doubled over in pain. She carefully took a couple of steps, sat down on the toilet seat, and waited for the pain to subside before standing. Walking out of the bathroom to where she laid down her purse Rose opened it and took out the pain medication. Tonight before going to bed she took two pills instead of one. She kept very quiet so as not to alert Russ while he slept in the room next to hers. It took her about two hours of tossing and turning before the pain went away and she was able to finally fall fast asleep.

Before The Flower Withers   *by Dennis C Mariotis*

CHAPTER 11
Freefalling

They took the next day very easy as they relaxed and enjoyed the beautiful sunny weather. Russ and Rose had a late breakfast served to them at the hotel's outdoor veranda. Afterwards they sat around the pool and basked in the sun for a while as they leisurely discussed the thrilling rides available in the area. Looking through the brochures

Before The Flower Withers   by Dennis C Mariotis

they picked up from the hotel lobby Rose made some very serious expressions. She turned the brochures up and down and sideways. Russ watched her and knew what she was thinking because he looked through them before she did.

Waiting for Rose to finish looking through all of them, Russ chuckled saying, "Those aren't like any rides we have in our neck of the woods, are they?" Rose shook her head and let out a long sigh before she answered, "No way! Is this stuff for real?" Nodding Russ replied, "Yes ma'am!" Rose shook her head and said, "These aren't rides! These are what they use to train astronauts before sending them into space! I can't believe people actually ride these things." Russ snickered and directed her attention as he pointed up at the top of the nearby hotel, "Look Rose. That's one of them right there!" Rose shaded her eyes from the sun with her hand as she looked up. With a look of disbelief she exclaimed, *"Holy crap!*

Before The Flower Withers   by Dennis C Mariotis

That's gotta be over six hundred feet high!" Russ corrected her, "Actually that's a little over nine hundred feet!" Unable to take her eyes off the ride Rose gasped, "What's the difference? Oh my God! Look at that! They're hanging off the side of the building and their spinning around nine hundred feet up without parachutes! If that thing snaps they'll all be Western Omelets when they land!" Sensing what he thought was fear in Rose he snickered asking, "So does that scare you enough to back out?"

Rose looked at him and shook her head, *"Hell no! That's getting me excited! I can't wait!* I can do that one as well as the roller coaster one where the roller coaster has over thirty feet of track over the side of a six hundred foot high building." Misreading her, Russ scratched his head and chuckled, "The way you looked I thought that ride scared you to death." Rose smiled at Russ, shook her head, shrugged her

Before The Flower Withers   by Dennis C Mariotis

shoulders, and replied, "Are you kidding? I'm not afraid of dying if that contraption snaps and falls to the ground." Chuckling she continued, **"It's what the splat's gonna feel like just before I exit this world that bothers the hell out of me***!"* That made Russ let out a loud laugh!

They spent the rest of the day talking about their lives and relaxing. Later on they enjoyed an evening dinner at the Mexican restaurant. After dinner they went to the lounge for a drink. There they discussed the next adventure awaiting Rose. She was so excited she even showed the waitress the picture in the brochure of what she was planning. The waitress looked and shivered as she told Rose that she was too scared to try something like that and just the thought of it sent chills through her body.

At a little after ten o'clock they walked to their respective rooms and retired for the night. Once again Rose experienced some deep pains.

Before The Flower Withers   by Dennis C Mariotis

They were not as bad as the previous night. This night she took one pain pill before laying down on her bed. Within about an hour she was asleep.

The next day Rose dressed in very light clothes and met Russ for a mid morning Continental breakfast. Rose didn't want to go on those thrill rides with a full stomach. Russ talked to her about what to expect since he experienced some very wild rides at the larger amusement parks he recently visited. As he was telling her about it, he noticed Rose was on her second glass of orange juice. After he finished his story he looked at her and smiled saying, "That's your second glass of orange juice."

Rose knew where he was going and replied, "Yes it is. Why do you ask?" Russ snickered and replied, "You usually have only one. Is there anything else in it?" Rose grinned and answered, "No Wallbangers, if that's what you're implying. I told you before they serve freshly squeezed orange juice and it tastes incredible. I'm

Before The Flower Withers   by Dennis C Mariotis

gonna be dizzy enough after being spun around at over nine hundred feet. The last thing anyone wants riding on that thing with me is an open regurgitating cocktail blender." Picturing Rose's description made Russ cringe and laugh. Shaking his head he responded, "Oh Rose. That's disgusting. But it would make for a great YouTube video. Just think about all the money they'd pay me for all the number of views I'd get for something like that!" Rose looked at him and said, "If that's what you want I suggest you do it yourself."

At about three o'clock that afternoon they arrived at the hotel that hosted the thrill rides. They took the elevator to the top and stood in line for Rose's ticket. Russ was not going to ride it. There was a long line of people waiting and it took about an hour for them to reach the ticket booth. Rose paid for her ticket, then she walked outside and stood in that line and waited for her turn to ride.

Before The Flower Withers   by Dennis C Mariotis

She watched several groups take their turn riding before it came time for her turn. Waiting for the people to exit she laughed at some of them as they went by. Most of them were laughing hysterically while others were upset with fear and attended to by their friends. Rose listened to the ride operator's instructions before her group boarded.

Looking at Russ who stood in the waiting area with his camera phone in hand she winked and waved at him. He smiled and waved back. When they boarded each person took a seat and was tended to by an employee who made sure each person's safety harness was secure. Sitting in the seat to Rose's right was a strapping middle aged macho type man. Making eye contact with him he laughed and with an arrogant tone he said to Rose, "*You're pretty old to be doing this. Are you sure you can handle it?*"

His rude comment got under her skin and aggravated her. Instead of returning the rudeness she

Before The Flower Withers   by Dennis C Mariotis

used sarcasm as she replied, "Mister! Last week I was at Fort Benning driving a tank and demonstrated to the soldiers how to fire large artillery shells at designated targets. Before that, in David and Goliath style, I knocked out the director of a very important event. And before that, I single handedly captured a dangerous armed robber for the Cobb County Sherriff's department. I'm just doing this to calm my nerves from all that other excitement. How about you? In a minute we're gonna be swinging around over nine hundred feet above the street with nothing between us but air. Are you sure *you* can handle it?" He shook his head and answered, "I don't believe that crap coming from an old lady. I'll bet you a hundred bucks this ride scares you so bad that you can't stand up straight when we're done!" Rose smiled and pointing her finger at him she said, *"You got a bet sonny boy!"*

Everyone on the ride braced as they felt it starting to move. It slowly lifted up and started to turn clockwise. When it reached a

Before The Flower Withers   by Dennis C Mariotis

certain height to where it cleared the area it gently moved outward. Within twenty seconds the machine's arm was fully extended outward from the building. Russ caught the action on his camera phone. Then the ride began to pick up speed until it reached its maximum speed. Most of the people riding were screaming and laughing. Rose was fascinated as she looked down and around. She smiled and felt as free as a bird. She had a look of sheer pleasure generated by the endorphins and the adrenalin rush from the excitement she was experiencing. Looking over at the wise ass macho man who bet she couldn't take it Rose began to laugh hysterically when she saw him. He looked like he was in shock. There was an incredible expression of fear in his face and all he did was look down at the street below. When the ride stopped turning clockwise it took about five seconds before it started to turn. This time it went counter clockwise. As it sped up Rose looked at the wise guy and almost felt sorry for him as he began to hyperventilate. Only now he

Before The Flower Withers   by Dennis C Mariotis

held his head up against the headrest. His eyes were closed and his mouth was wide open. Rose couldn't help herself as she laughed and yelled to him, *"Hey sonny boy! Close your mouth, there're buzzards flying over your head!"*

The ride lasted about ten minutes before the spinning slowed down and stopped. Dangling over the side of the building the ride made a couple of deliberate jerks up and down. This gave the impression that there was a problem. The people on the ride continued with their laughing and screaming. Rose checked on the wise guy and laughed when she saw that sometime during the last minute of the ride, he fainted and sat limp in the seat with his eyes closed and his spit drooling out the side of his mouth. Rose couldn't resist as she took out her phone and snapped a picture of him.

The ride finally ended as the arm fully retracted and set the ride down and secured it to a locked position. When the operator cleared the workers to assist the passengers

Before The Flower Withers   by Dennis C Mariotis

disembark the ride they unharnessed everyone. Walking off under her own power Rose kept her smile all the way out. After explaining to Russ about the wise guy, she and Russ waited outside the exit gate. The last one to leave was the wise guy. It took two of his buddies to hold him up and walk him off the ride. He was conscious but very weak kneed. As they walked past Rose he strained his eyes and looked at her as if he didn't remember her.

Rose smiled at the wise guy and asked, *"Remember me? I'm the old lady who sat next to you and I have video of you squealing and passing out tough guy! You also bet me a hundred dollars that I was gonna do what you're doing at the end of the ride. Well?"* Looking at her he shook his head and let go of one of his friends. Putting his hand in his pocket he pulled out a hundred dollar bill. Handing it to her he said, "Lady? I can't believe it!" Holding the money, before taking it out of his hand she smiled and asked him, "Double or nothing?" The wise guy thought about it and immediately shook

Before The Flower Withers   by Dennis C Mariotis

his head and said, *"Oh Hell no!"* Letting go of the bill his friends assisted him all the way into the building.

As they watched them walk off, Russ asked Rose, "I wonder why a guy like that was so scared?" They laughed when Rose answered, "Apparently, **he** has something to live for!" Russ gave her a hug and said, "I got a bunch of pictures. You did great." Rose looked at the ride, then over the rail at the street nine hundred feet below and said, "I felt great. Like an angel who just got her wings and flying in Heaven." They laughed with Russ' response, "I saw that in your face. As for that wise guy, he must've felt like he was in the *other* place!" Rose laughed and said, "He did look like hell, didn't he?" Arm in arm they walked into the building and took the elevator down to the ground level. They spent the rest of the day riding around the town and talking about the other items on her list.

Before The Flower Withers   by Dennis C Mariotis

CHAPTER 12
Born To Be Wild!

Not satisfied with her wild ride yesterday, Rose woke up the next morning feeling better than she did the last couple of days. Falling asleep last night she didn't need any pain medication, but she was feeling weaker every day. Hiding all her pain and weakness from Russ she rolled over and got out of bed.

Before The Flower Withers   by Dennis C Mariotis

Stretching and yawning all the way to the bathroom she washed her face and brushed her teeth. Then she walked around the room a couple of times to get the stiffness out of her body. Hearing Russ in the next room she decided to get dressed and wait for him to call her for breakfast.

Within half an hour Rose stood up and walked to the door connecting the rooms and opened the door after hearing Russ knocking on it. Opening the door Rose grinned when she saw Russ' expression. He looked like he had a rough night. "Well good morning honey. You look all tuckered out." said Rose. Finishing his long yawn he replied as he rubbed his eyes, "Oh yeah! I tossed and turned all night from those crazy dreams. Every time I fell asleep I dreamt about you falling out of that damn ride, and I was helpless as I watched you fall all the way down. But I woke up before you hit the ground." Rose laughed and said, "I dreamt about the ride but I slept just fine. Let's get some breakfast. You look like you need a pot of coffee."

Before The Flower Withers   *by Dennis C Mariotis*

Russ nodded as they exited through his room and out to the hallway where they took the elevator down to the restaurant level.

Sitting down to breakfast neither one of them had an appetite. Rose told the waitress to bring them the Continental breakfast. It consisted of coffee, orange juice, and a couple of blueberry muffins. They talked about the next item on the list. A ride on a motorcycle. Rose had some anxiety about this one though but she was also excited about it. Russ saw this in her eyes and asked, "Is there anything wrong?" She shook her head and looked at her coffee before answering him, "I'm a little concerned with those things. I mean the thought of it is thrilling but riding down the road without any metal protection around me like a car is pretty scary."

Russ tried to comfort her by showing her the brochure and reassuring her of the safety addressed in it, "I wouldn't worry about that Rose. See? It says here that this

Before The Flower Withers   by Dennis C Mariotis

company has an excellent record for safety and customer satisfaction. We can go to this place and look around and if you don't like what you see, we can go somewhere else. There's about ten of these places here. I'm sure we'll find one you like." She nodded and smiled. Feeling better she said, "That sounds great." Looking down at the half eaten muffins Rose said, "I didn't have much of an appetite for breakfast. Let's ride around and check out these places and decide on which one after lunch. Okay?" Russ nodded, then he stood up and followed Rose out of the restaurant to the elevator.

        In a few minutes they were out the door and in a cab riding along the strip. They had the cab driver take them around to several places. The driver waited for them while they looked around and checked out the businesses. After looking at four of these places they finally got hungry for lunch. Requesting the driver to drop them off at a local diner he did so. Even though it was a little out of the way off the main Vegas strip he

Before The Flower Withers   *by Dennis C Mariotis*

assured them it would be easy for them to call a cab.

After paying the driver, Rose and Russ exited the cab which dropped them off at the far end of the diner's parking lot. It was a short walk to the entrance. Walking through the parking lot they noticed about half of the vehicles were motorcycles. Rose turned to Russ and said, "I bet you the people in this place could recommend a good place for me to get a motorcycle ride." Russ hesitated as he nodded. Entering the restaurant they looked around. Most of the patrons were bikers having lunch or just sitting around drinking beer.

With some apprehension in his voice Russ whispered to Rose, "This looks like a pretty rough place. I think we ought to leave and go back to the hotel for lunch." Rose looked at him and shook her head saying, "Oh nonsense! Relax. These look like perfectly nice young men stopping by to have lunch." Looking around for a table she pointed and said, "Let's go sit at

Before The Flower Withers   by Dennis C Mariotis

that booth over there." Russ looked at the booth but to his surprise, sitting at the booth next to it were three really tough looking bikers. Pretending like it didn't bother him Russ walked behind Rose who sat down first. Russ hid his nervousness as he sat down with his back to the bikers.

Picking up on his anxiety Rose asked, "Are you okay honey?" Russ stuttered a little answering, "Oh. Oh yeah. I...I'm fine. Let's order." Everyone in the place stayed pretty much to themselves. There were no problems or anything to be alarmed about. But Russ was still apprehensive about being surrounded by these big strapping brutes. He was no match for them and he knew it very well. The lunch, obviously not a five star cuisine, was actually very good considering it was an off the beaten path greasy spoon.

As they finished their meal Rose looked at Russ and said, "Wow! That was a surprisingly good meal!" Russ nodded, "I have to say, it

Before The Flower Withers   by Dennis C Mariotis

was better than the lunch we had at that five star place in the hotel!" Overhearing their comments, one of the bikers from the booth behind Russ stood up and came to their table. Looking down at the table Russ saw the lower half of the biker's body as he walked to them and stopped. Russ slowly looked up and hiding his fear he made eye contact with the muscular biker. Rose saw him walk over and smiled at him. From a stern expression the biker smiled at her and said, "I'm one of the owners here and I heard what you both said about my place."

Russ tensed up for a moment but then was relieved to hear the biker continue, "My name is Percival Johnson but you can call me *Stoner* and I want to thank you for the compliments." Rose smiled and replied, "You're welcome. My name is Rose and this is my grandson Russ." Stoner grinned at her and said, "Well if there's anything else we can get for you let us know. I hope to see you again."

Before The Flower Withers   by Dennis C Mariotis

Before he turned to leave Rose stopped him, "Mr. Stoner? There is one thing I'd like to ask you." Stoner grinned at Rose and waited for her to ask. She asked, "You ride motorcycles and you own this restaurant so you know a lot about the people in this community. I've looked around today for a business that offers thrilling motorcycle rides. So far I don't like what I've seen. Can you recommend anyone please?" Stoner pursed his lips and scratched his chin as he thought about her question. Then he looked at Rose and said, "How serious are you about taking a bike ride?" Rose nodded and answered, "I'm very serious! You see, I only have a few more months to live and it's one of those things I wanna do before I leave this world." With a serious expression Stoner replied, "Wait. I wanna talk to my partners. I'll be right back."

Stoner signaled his two partners at the booth to join him in a private conversation. Rose and Russ glanced at them while they waited. They could not hear their conversation but

Before The Flower Withers   by Dennis C Mariotis

they did see them nodding and looking back at Rose. Finally Stoner and his partners stood up and walked over to the table to talk to Rose. Stoner said, "Rose and Russ, is it?" Russ nodded, Stoner continued, "I'd like to introduce you to my partners." Pointing to one and then the other they nodded as Stoner continued, "These are my brothers. This is Garth and this ugly guy here is Boots."

Stoner turned to address Russ, "We need to speak to Rose privately so I need you to wait by that back door marked Private until we're done." Russ looked at Rose who nodded, then turned to Stoner and said, "Okay." After Russ stood up and walked to the door marked Private and waited, Stoner and his brothers Garth and Boots sat down at the booth with Rose. Russ watched them but was unable to pick up on the conversation. He was relieved to see Rose and the bikers smiling and nodding. Rose was pretty animated as she explained her situation to the bikers.

Before The Flower Withers   by Dennis C Mariotis

About fifteen minutes later they finished their conversation. Exiting the booth the bikers waited for Rose to get up. She followed them to where Russ was standing. Stoner pulled out his keys and opened the door to the back room. Walking in Stoner turned on the light. There was another room located to the right and down a short corridor. Stoner had Russ sit on his desk chair while he sat in front of him. Garth and Boots took Rose and walked around the corner and into the side room. They didn't close the door so Russ was able to hear their entire conversation but was unable to see what was going on in that room between Rose, Garth, and Boots.

Russ sat nervously behind the desk. Looking at Stoner he asked, "What's going on?" Stoner replied, "Just relax and take it easy. We told Rose that bikers take riding very seriously. Riding is a religion to us. It's not something you just decide to do one day." Russ was antsy but he didn't want to cross the bikers. He couldn't fight his way out with one of

Before The Flower Withers   by Dennis C Mariotis

them, let alone three street hardened muscular rough riders. He asked, "So what does that have to do with Rose?" Stoner answered, "She told us about her Bucket List and we told her about the initiation she has to go through if she wants us to give her a thrilling bike ride." Russ asked, "You're not gonna do anything to hurt her are you?" Stoner smiled and leaned his head back and answered, "She agreed, so we'll see how much she can take. Just wait and don't move from there. They'll be done in about fifteen minutes." Russ nodded. Stoner saw the tenseness in Russ' face and his shallow breathing as he stared at Stoner.

Hearing a low humming sound Russ turned his head towards the room and with concern in his voice he asked Stoner, "What's that noise?" Stoner grinned and said, "That's part of the initiation process." Not being able to see what was going on with Rose, Russ tensed up even more when he heard the voices coming from the room.

Before The Flower Withers   by Dennis C Mariotis

The conversation coming from the room went like this:

GARTH: Okay Rose. This is for you. Now take your top off.

ROSE: Okay. Wow! That's so big. Do you think it's gonna fit?

GARTH: Yeah! Relax. I've done this lots of times. Just hold still and be calm otherwise it's gonna hurt. Good. Here it goes.

ROSE: (moans) Ouch! Take it easy. Ooo! That's better. Mm!

GARTH: There you go. You're doing fine. Wow. You can really take it. Some women don't stop screaming!

ROSE: (moans) Ooo. That's really a different sensation than I ever felt before.

Russ was shaking with fear at the conversation. All he heard for the next five minutes was Rose letting out low moaning sounds. Then he heard Garth speaking.

Before The Flower Withers   by Dennis C Mariotis

GARTH: Wow! I'm done. You were great!

ROSE: Now that was an experience I never had before! And it did hurt quite a bit.

GARTH: Okay....Boots? She all yours!

Russ was panicking as he sat there. Wild and crazy thoughts went through his mind. Stoner just sat there thumbing through a biker's magazine. Then Russ jerked his head back towards the room as he heard the conversation pick up.

BOOTS: Hey Rose. Look at what I got for you!

ROSE: Where are you gonna put that?

BOOTS: Your ass! Now bend over like a good girl.

Russ was petrified. Stoner chuckled seeing Russ turning beet red with sweat pouring down his face.

ROSE: That's not as big as Garth's. Is it gonna hurt?

***Before The Flower Withers** by Dennis C Mariotis*

BOOTS: Like Garth's it's gonna hurt a little at first but the pain will be a lot less after I continue for a few minutes.

ROSE: Oh Boots. Be gentle.

BOOTS: Hahaha! Gentle is my middle name. Here we go. Now don't move!

ROSE: Ouch! Oooo! That hurt. Take it easy.

BOOTS: Butts are very sensitive areas. Relax I'm almost there!

Russ stood up when he heard Rose but one look at Stoner who signaled him to sit down and he sat down. Russ listened as he was still sweating and nervous. In about five minutes of Rose's low moans and an occasional 'Ouch,' they were done.

BOOTS: There....Okay, I'm done. Now relax while Garth cleans you up.

ROSE: Wow! I'm glad that's over with!

BOOTS: Yeah! But you'll be a little sore when we take you on that ride.

Before The Flower Withers   by Dennis C Mariotis

Russ was relieved when Boots walked out of the room and joined him in the office. Stoner asked Boots, "How did it go?" Boots nodded, "She was good. She took it like a trooper from both of us!" Boots looked at Russ and smiled, "You should be proud of her!" Russ couldn't hold back and with anger in his voice he said, "Proud of her after what you guys just did to her? You guys took advantage of an old lady whose terminally ill and gonna die, and you're telling me I should be proud? You're sick and you should be horsewhipped." Stoner looked at Boots and they both couldn't hold it any more as they busted out with loud laughter.

Seeing them laughing angered Russ even more, "You guys think this is funny? Someone should do what you did to your grandmother. Then I'd like to see you laugh, you, you assholes!" Boots and Stoner laughed even louder. Russ demanded, "Where is she? I need to get her home now. This whole Bucket List is all my fault. Shit!" Hearing footsteps coming from the room Russ waited. Boots spoke up,

Before The Flower Withers   by Dennis C Mariotis

"Garth just finished cleaning her off. Here she comes now."

Walking around the corner and coming into view was Rose with a big smile on her face and Garth walking into the room behind her. She looked at Russ, and seeing him sweaty and angry looking concerned her. Her smile changed to a concerned cringe as she asked, "Russ? What's wrong honey?" Russ stared at her and with anger and confusion in his voice he said, *"Grandma, are you all right?! I heard all your painful moaning and groaning! What the hell did they do to you?"*

Understanding what Russ misinterpreted by the conversation he overheard, Rose, in sync with Garth, Boots, and Stoner, broke out into hearty laughter. She asked, *"What did you think they were doing?"* Russ was thoroughly confused and answered, "Well I thought they were...well you know!"

Stoner interrupted him and with a stern look and firm voice he backed Russ down, "Did you think they were raping your grandmother? We have

Before The Flower Withers   by Dennis C Mariotis

grandmothers too! And we love them! And if anyone laid an unkind hand on them we wouldn't be sitting behind a desk sweating our asses off." Russ answered, "What did you expect me to do? Fight three gorillas that would have torn me apart?" Boots looked at his brothers, then they looked at Russ and all three nodded their heads as Boots chimed in, "Well yeah!"

Russ threw up his hands and sighed. Confused he asked Rose, "Well what did they do to you in that room?" Rose smiled and stepped back. Picking up her blouse she said, "Look Russ. Isn't it beautiful and so cool?" Russ looked and to his surprise he saw what Garth did. It was a beautiful red rose tattooed on her chest just above her breasts but far enough below her neckline that could not be seen under her blouse. Russ nodded and breathed a sigh of relief and said, "A tattoo. That explains the sounds that I heard. But what about what Boots did to your butt?"

***Before The Flower Withers**   by Dennis C Mariotis*

Turning her left hip to Russ she picked up her skirt and pulled down her panties far enough to reveal another tattoo of a Rose on her butt cheek. This one was smaller but it's also a masterpiece. Russ looked up and shook his head. Then with a blank stare he looked at all of them for about five seconds. Then Russ started to chuckle and soon his chuckle turned into hysterical laughter. They all joined in and laughter filled the room for about two minutes. Russ rubbed his head as he walked up to Rose and gave her a tight hug. Then he looked at her and they both laughed while they hugged each other.

Calming down after their hearty laughter, Stoner looked at Russ and Rose and said, "Well Rose? You're officially initiated into our gang, The Badasses! Are you ready for a real ride with me on my Harley?" She smiled and said, "Sure. Can Russ come along?" Boots snickered and chimed in, "Sure. Why not? He's a pretty good grandson to do what he's doing for you. Come on...let's hit the road!"

Before The Flower Withers   by Dennis C Mariotis

Rose walked out of the room with Stoner. He took her outside to his motorcycle and instructed her on how to hold on to him and where to keep her feet so that the exhaust does not burn her. After about ten minutes Russ, Boots and Garth walked out and joined them. Rose said, "I was wondering when you were going to join us. What kept you?" Russ smiled as he pulled up his sleeve. Showing Rose his tattoo of a rose on his upper arm with the words, 'Shotgun Grandma Rose - Forever' encircling it, she proudly smiled. Russ said, "Now I'm initiated!'

It took about ten minutes for Boots to explain to Russ what to do while riding behind him. Then with a loud thunderous sound Boots cranked up his bike and took off with Russ sitting on the seat right behind him and holding on for dear life. Within three minutes Stoner had Rose seated and buckled in and with a helmet on her he cranked up his bike. At first he took it slow but Rose urged him to speed up. Riding down the highway Russ experienced the adrenaline rush of

Before The Flower Withers   by Dennis C Mariotis

excitement from the feeling on the motorcycle speeding down the road at over ninety miles per hour. Looking back he saw a motorcycle in the distance. He wondered how Rose was doing and he was somewhat concerned knowing Rose was apprehensive about riding fast on a motorcycle from their earlier conversation.

They traveled almost thirty miles when Russ yelled to Boots, "Boots. Do you wanna slow down so Stoner and Rose can catch up to us?" Boots laughed and yelled back, "Look behind you!" Russ looked at the road behind him and smiled as he was surprised to see Stoner traveling faster than Boots and coming up on his left. Within a minute Stoner was even with Boots. Rose smiled at him and gave Russ the thumbs up. Russ was very happy for her. Then Rose yelled to Stoner, *"Faster baby, faster!"* Stoner nodded, then twisting the bike's throttle the engine roared and they took off. Russ laughed when he heard Rose yelling, *"Woooo Hooooo!"* as they drove off.

Before The Flower Withers   by Dennis C Mariotis

An hour later Boots and Stoner arrived at the hotel to drop them off after their long ride. They laughed at Russ and Rose as they had a very hard time getting off the bikes. They also laughed at the difficulty with the simple act of walking. Boots snickered and said, "We told you, you were gonna have a hard time walking. It's like riding a skidoo or a horse for a couple of hours for the first time."

It took them a couple of minutes to get their bearings but Rose and Russ straightened up. Before getting back on their bikes, Boots and Stoner shook Russ' hand and wished him well and invited him back anytime. But when it came time to say good bye to Rose the two muscular men had a hard time. They took turns hugging her and apologized that Garth didn't make it because he had a real soft heart for Rose since they recently lost one of their grandmothers.

Hugging her Stoner said, "Good bye Rose. I had a great time and

Before The Flower Withers   by Dennis C Mariotis

I'll never forget you!" Then Boots held her and when he let go he said, "We'll meet again someday when I get my wings. Until then I'll never forget this time together and your cute butt cheek where I put my mark! And I especially won't forget Russ' reaction. Boy did he give us a story to tell our group tonight!" When they got on their bikes they took a moment to wipe their eyes as they watched Russ walk with Rose into the hotel before driving away.

Rose and Russ stopped and sat down in the hotel lounge for a cocktail before going to their rooms. Rose sat down very slowly and moaned all the way, "Ooooo! That smarts." Russ asked, "I know that ride cramped some muscles in places that I thought I never felt before." Rose replied, "It's not from the ride. Mine's from the needlework. Ouch!" Russ snickered and said, "Well we can check two more things off your list Rose!" She smiled and said, "Yes. But you know what I'm feeling Russ?" He shook his head, "No. What's that?" She sighed and explained, "When the doctor gave me the bad news,

Before The Flower Withers   *by Dennis C Mariotis*

I didn't feel as bad as I thought I would if I ever was given that kind of news. But now, after doing all these things, and meeting all these people, I have some very strong mixed feelings. I'm feeling glad that there's an end in sight for these terrible pains I've been going through. But at the same time I'm feeling miserable that I'm gonna miss the fun times like this as well as seeing you go on with your life." Russ felt bad and with empathy he said, "I'm sorry Rose. You know I also have mixed feelings. I feel great knowing you're having a great time. But I also feel bad knowing that this is gonna come to an end real soon."

Looking at Russ she said, "I want this day to end on a good note. Let's have a few more drinks and stay here until they start the Karaoke. We can sing a duet!" Russ smiled and said, "It's a deal. Just keep your bra where it is!" They laughed when Rose said, "Okay, but I'm gonna show them my new big rose and then I'm gonna show them my little rose." Russ laughed as he waved to the waitress to bring them

Before The Flower Withers   by Dennis C Mariotis

another round." Turning to Rose he said, "Don't worry Rose. I'll never be depressed with all the great memories filled with fun and never a dull moment that we've made together." With that they raised their glasses and touched them together in a silent toast, before taking another drink.

CHAPTER 13
Rose Meets Barney

On their last day in Las Vegas, Russ and Rose had their usual breakfast together. Russ' job was to ensure Rose was feeling up for another bucket list event, and Rose was just glad to feel well enough to go about the day under her own strength after another evening episode of pain and discomfort. Stirring her tea Rose

Before The Flower Withers   by Dennis C Mariotis

stared off as she thought about the things to come. Seeing the faraway look in her eyes Russ interrupted and broke her thoughts when he asked, "Anything wrong?"

She blinked and looked at Russ, grinned, and answered, "Oh no. I was just thinking about everything. Thanks for snapping me out of my thoughts of tomorrow and bringing me back to the reality of today." Russ grinned as he put down his coffee cup. Clearing his throat after he swallowed he said, "Today's our last day here and I want to be sure you're up for our trip to the circus."

Rose smiled answering, "I'm ready." She chuckled as she thought about an incident with Russ when he was a child. Then she opened up and shared that fond memory, "I remember the first time I took you to the circus. You were three years old. You did great! Up until the time the clowns came up to you and scared the hell out of you." Russ snickered, "They still do. Well then what did I do?"

Before The Flower Withers   by Dennis C Mariotis

Rose looked up and snickered as she recalled the vivid details of the images from that time. Then she looked at Russ and laughed as she explained, "You screamed bloody murder! Then you climbed up from my lap and over my shoulder so fast, and you didn't stop until you were on my back and holding on with a death grip around my neck, just like a trained monkey. The people around us got a bigger kick watching you instead of watching the circus."

Russ laughed as he listened to her telling that story. He also knew this was a good distraction for Rose to have her mind on things other than her cancer. Listening to her, Rose continued, "You kept screaming so loud right in my ear! It took me two days for the ringing in my ear to stop. You finally came down after the clowns left. You kept your eyes fixated on them and every time they came anywhere near us, you screamed. The man from the family sitting next to us bought you an ice cream cone. That calmed you down." Russ chuckled, "That was nice of him." Rose

Before The Flower Withers   by Dennis C Mariotis

shook her head and quickly replied, "He didn't do that because of his kindness. He did that to shut you up because you were distracting them from enjoying the show. After you finished the ice cream you were so exhausted that you fell asleep almost immediately and slept through the rest of the circus acts. The elephants didn't even wake you up." Russ made her laugh when he asked, "Do you think that guy put anything in the ice cream to knock me out?" Rose snickered answering, "If he didn't I would've!"

They laughed as Rose told him other stories from his childhood. Finishing their breakfast they left the hotel and walked outside where he hailed a cab. Russ instructed the driver to take them to the circus. Twenty six miles later they arrived. Exiting the cab they looked around at the huge canvas enclosed Big Top. Walking to the ticket booth they purchased front row seats and entered the tented stage to see the show.

Before The Flower Withers   *by Dennis C Mariotis*

Once inside they took their seats and watched. The sights, sounds, tastes, and smells of popcorn, cracker jack, and of course, the animals brought back so many memories that flooded their minds as they recalled events they thought they forgot about many years ago. Rose laughed hysterically when Russ pretended to be scared out of his wits as he screamed and hugged Rose's neck when the clowns came up to them. She made Russ laugh when she turned to him and told him not to climb up on her lap and over her shoulders.

Two hours of circus acts seemed to go by quickly. When the show ended three of the animal trainers came out with their animals and waited in the separate circus rings. Here they offered the crowd a chance to either ride or pet the animal, for a price of course. Rose and Russ left their seats and waited for their turn in line after buying tickets to see these exotic creatures. The first one was a baby lion cub. The trainer instructed Rose to sit down and gently scratch its

Before The Flower Withers   by Dennis C Mariotis

head. Russ stood by and took pictures, then he took his turn and sat down next to the cub and scratched its head.

Moving on to the next animal Rose cringed when it was her turn to meet Sally, the twelve foot albino python. The trainers held onto the long snake and carefully draped it around Rose's neck and shoulders. She sat very still and breathed very deeply as she clenched her teeth. It was cold but not slimy like she thought it would be. Russ took more pictures as he laughed at Rose's expressions. It didn't bother Russ when it came for his turn. He was desensitized to pythons because his friends had them as pets and they let him handle them.

Next came the treat for both of them. It was a ride on Barney the large African elephant. They were both anxious to ride Barney as they witnessed how powerful yet how gentle the creature was with the riders in front of them. When it came their turn to ride him, the trainer instructed them on what to do. One of the things

Before The Flower Withers   by Dennis C Mariotis

the trainer emphasized was to avoid touching Barney's ears because they are very sensitive. Nodding their heads in understanding, Rose was then assisted up and sat on Barney for about ten seconds while Russ took a few pictures. Then he climbed up and sat behind her. Rose sat on the edge of Barney's neck. Russ braced himself then he held onto Rose. When they were ready they gave the trainer the thumbs up sign.

Seeing they were ready the trainer began to walk and guide Barney's steps gently and carefully around the designated area. Rose looked over her shoulder at Russ and said, "This is really neat. It reminds me of riding on top of that tank." Rose shook her head and sighed. Then she laughed when Russ snickered and replied, "Yeah. But this one's safer. Its turret eats peanuts!"

About two minutes into their three minute ride Rose looked over at Russ and said, "Barney sure flaps his ears a lot. A couple of times he hit my leg real hard." Russ asked,

Before The Flower Withers   by Dennis C Mariotis

"Did it hurt?" Rose shook her head answering, "No. But I don't believe that garbage about how sensitive his ears are. I'm guessing that's some old wives tale!" Russ replied, "I don't know and while we're riding this twelve thousand pound beast, I sure don't want to find out."

Rose shook her head and peered at Russ and said, "Oh come on! Where's your sense of adventure? Here! Watch!" Reaching and firmly grabbing Barney's ear as it flapped against her leg, Russ nervously and loudly yelled in Rose's ear, **"No don't. Let it go!"** Rose held on tight and gave Barney's ear a firm tug and twist. That changed Rose's belief...And very quickly too.

Rose let go but not before Barney's immediate reaction. The animal suddenly stopped and reared up on its hind legs and let out a loud trumpet distress sound which got everyone's attention. Recognizing Barney's painful call his trainer along with his assistants took action and tried to comfort Barney as his front

Before The Flower Withers   by Dennis C Mariotis

legs came down to the ground. The trainer screamed momentarily as he pulled his foot away from under Barney's left leg. Most of the people ran outside to safety. This startled the python so bad that it tightened its grip around the man's torso and quickly began to squeeze. The handlers were struggling but managed to pull it off him. The lion cub jumped on its trainer and hid its head under his arm.

Getting back to the scene on top of Barney, Rose had an expression of near shock as her eyes bulged. She held onto the rope with all her strength while Russ held onto the rope with one hand and onto Rose with the other. Except for Russ, no one else saw what Rose did.

It took about thirty seconds for Barney to calm down. The trainer grimaced from the pain in his foot but took the time to guide the elephant back to the stand where Russ and Rose carefully climbed off Barney's back and stepped down to ground level. Rose looked around and seeing the

Before The Flower Withers   by Dennis C Mariotis

medics surrounding Barney's trainer she walked up to see the damage. Seeing her the trainer said, "I'm sorry about that. I don't know what got into Barney. The last time he did that is when he saw a mouse. Elephants are afraid of mice getting into their ears. Anyway, are you okay lady?"

Rose nodded and pretended as if she was an innocent victim of circumstance and answered, "I'm fine. I don't have the slightest idea what happened either. Maybe it was another mouse. But I'm concerned about you. Are you gonna be okay?" Russ pursed his lips and whispered in her ear, "Yeah. It was a mouse all right. A mouse named Rose! You big fibber!" Rose turned to Russ and whispered back, "Shuddup! You wanna get us in trouble? Leave everything well enough alone." The trainer looked at Rose and said, "Thanks for your concern. This is not the first time Barney smashed my foot. It's an occupational hazard with elephants. I'll be all right. Thank you again for your concern." Rose smiled as

Before The Flower Withers   by Dennis C Mariotis

she turned to Russ and whispered, "Hurry up. Let's get outta here!"

Hooking his arm she pulled him as she walked faster than he did. He laughed and said, "What's your rush?" She laughed and said, "Don't you know anything about elephants?" Russ chuckled as he answered with sarcasm, "Yes! I found out today the best way to test an elephant's ear sensitivity!" Rose chuckled and said as she stepped up the pace until they were finally outside, "Okay wise ass. Don't you know elephants have a great memory?" Russ answered, "Yeah. I learned about that. So what?" Rose stopped and looked into Russ' eyes and firmly stated, "I was afraid Barney would run after me and trample us when he saw me and remembered that I was the one who twisted his ear!" Russ laughed and said, "That's ridiculous!" Suddenly they both bolted to the parking lot when they heard Barney sounding his loud trumpet from inside the circus area. Rushing forward Rose yelled at Russ, "See? I told you!"

***Before The Flower Withers**   by Dennis C Mariotis*

Reaching the parking lot they walked to the taxi cab stand area and quickly boarded a cab. Once safely inside Rose turned to Russ and said, "That was an experience!" Russ nodded and laughed. Then, after about a minute he laughed again only this time out loud. Rose asked, "What's so funny?" His witty remark made Rose laugh out loud, "I was just thinking about the time we wrote up your bucket list. You told me that you were sorry the things you agreed to do weren't the most sophisticated or the most exciting things." Rose replied, "Yeah. So?" Russ shook his head and said, "At first I agreed with you. But after doing everything so far, I think you made the best choices. Everything you chose you made them more exciting than I ever could've imagined!" Rose nodded and chuckled, "Come to think of it; I believe you're right. I don't think we would have had anywhere near this much fun doing all that other stuff!"

Arriving back at the hotel, they exited the cab and walked into the building. First they went to

Before The Flower Withers   by Dennis C Mariotis

their respective rooms where they showered, changed, and packed their bags so they would not be rushed the next morning when they checked out of the hotel and flew back home. Rose rested for a couple of hours after feeling tired from the exciting events at the circus. She also needed to take her pain medication as her pains were now more frequent and more painful. She slept for a couple of hours while Russ took the time to download all the pictures and watch television. When Rose awakened she called on Russ and together they went to the restaurant for dinner. After dinner they went to the lounge to celebrate their last night in Las Vegas before retiring for the evening.

Before The Flower Withers   by Dennis C Mariotis

CHAPTER 14
Comin' 'Round The Mountain!

Arriving back home to Georgia after spending two very fun filled memorable weeks in Las Vegas, Russ and Rose took a couple of days off to catch up on some personal things. The third day home Russ visited Rose to check up on her and discuss her final bucket list items. In a familiar scene,

Before The Flower Withers   by Dennis C Mariotis

Russ and Rose are sitting around her kitchen table as they are finishing up a piece of Rose's incredible cheesecake. Rose thanked Russ for picking up the dishes and putting them in the dishwasher. When he came back to the table he sat down to continue going over the next bucket list item.

Russ reached over and picking up a brochure he opened it and showed it to Rose. He pointed to it and said, "Here grandma. This is the place that offers some of the best and safest mountain climbing, and it's located in Helen, Georgia. Look. Doesn't that look exciting?" Rose looked at the pictures in the brochure and shook her head and said, "Wow! Those are pretty rocky places. I sure wouldn't wanna fall down once I climbed up there! When do you wanna do this?" Russ answered, "We can do it any day you want. It's only about an hour and a half drive from here so we can easily do it in a day."

Russ looked up the company's website on his cell phone and searched for their schedule. Looking up

Before The Flower Withers   by Dennis C Mariotis

the available days he put his phone down and said, to Rose, "They're open tomorrow then they're closed for the following two days." Looking at the brochure for a few more seconds, Rose set it down and said, "Tomorrow would probably be the best for two reasons. One, I'm pretty much rested, and two, the weather's gonna be good through tomorrow, but they're expecting rain off and on for the next week. Besides my pains are becoming more unbearable and the medicine is not helping like it did before."

Russ grew more concerned as, once again, the reality of the situation resurfaced. He sighed then turned and smiled as he changed his demeanor and said, "I'll pick you up tomorrow morning so we can be the first group to climb. I know you're at your peak in the morning after you've had your orange juice." She smiled at him and replied, "You're right. You wouldn't want me trying to climb a rocky mountain later on after I have my (she winked at him) *'other'* orange juice!" Her humor lifted his spirit as

Before The Flower Withers   by Dennis C Mariotis

he winked at her and said, "I don't know grandma. Maybe you should wait until later on after you had a few of those *other* orange juices. Then you'd be able to climb higher if you were already high when you started!" They laughed as Russ stood up and hugged Rose before leaving. Russ took a few steps towards the front door and stopped when he heard Rose yell for him. Thinking it was an emergency he quickly stopped, turned around and ran to her side in the kitchen.

Seeing that she was all right and just rummaging through her purse he calmed down and said, "Grandma. I'm glad to see you're okay. The way you yelled I thought you were having a stroke! Please don't do that again." Rose gently grasped his arm and said, "Oh forgive me! I'm so sorry I startled you like that. But I just remembered that I picked up a couple of souvenirs for you while we were in Vegas and I didn't want to forget to give them to you." Russ snickered and said, "Thanks grandma but you didn't have to do that. The memories are all I

Before The Flower Withers **by Dennis C Mariotis**

needed." Rose pulled out an envelope and opening it she pulled out the two checks from the casino and showing them to Russ she nonchalantly pretended it was nothing major and said, "Oh really? Then I guess I can give these to somebody else."

Russ' eyes bulged and his jaw dropped when he saw that both checks had his name on them. He stood there motionless and almost in shock before he snapped out of it and excitedly stuttered incoherently, "B... b.. b.. I mean, g...g...grandma!" Rose laughed and interrupted him, "That's not very intelligent coming from a grad student. All that college and all you can say is B..b..b when I'm giving you almost ninety thousand dollars? Is that something else from your generation that needs translation into my generation? Here take it! It's yours! But think about it before you speak." She chuckled as she handed him the checks.

Russ slowly put his hand out and accepted them. With his jaw

Before The Flower Withers   by Dennis C Mariotis

still dropped and his eyebrows raised he looked at them and swallowed before coming out of his shocked expression and spoke, "Sorry grandma. I didn't expect anything like this. How did they let you put my name on it too? After all, those are your winnings!" Rose was overjoyed with his reaction. Then she calmly replied, "I had this planned all along when I had you sign that paperwork with me. I told you that you had to sign as a witness, but you didn't realize that you signed as a co-winner with me. That's why your name is on the check next to mine. I already endorsed the check. All you have to do is put it in your bank for your future."

Overcome with excitement Russ hugged Rose and kissed her check and said, "Thank you so much grandma, but I didn't do all this with you for money." Rose looked at him and answered, "I know you didn't. You did this because you love me and you have a big heart." Her voice cracked and her eyes welled up with tears as she continued, "And I wanted to give you

Before The Flower Withers   by Dennis C Mariotis

something for all the time you took doing all this for me and making me so happy." She sniffled and continued, "And if it wasn't for you telling me to take my winnings off the Craps table, I would have lost it all. Then I won again at Roulette using your birthday. What I left for you in my Will is not much. After winning this I wanted to be sure that you really knew how much you mean to me. It's not about the money. It's about what you did! If anyone asks you, tell them you had an amazing lucky streak in Las Vegas. And that's the truth. You were my good luck man! The players at the table called me their *Lucky Lady*. But to me, you were my *Lucky Man!*"

        Russ folded the checks and taking out his wallet he carefully placed them in it and returned it to his back pocket. Then he looked at Rose and nodded as he hugged her and kissed her cheek again. Letting go and before turning to leave he gently wiped a tear from her eye with his thumb. Unable to speak he sniffled as his lips quivered. Rose grinned and letting him

Before The Flower Withers   by Dennis C Mariotis

go she said, "It's okay. Now go on home and get some rest. We've got a mountain to climb tomorrow!" Russ managed to return the grin as he wiped his eyes before turning and walking out of the kitchen and exited the house.

      The next morning Russ showed up at Rose's house at seven o'clock. Rose was all ready to go as she opened the door and walked out to him. She greeted him with a hug and kiss on the cheek before locking the front door. Russ walked very carefully with her down the front porch steps and to his car where helped her in and closed the door. After walking around to the driver's side he entered his car and within a couple of minutes he drove off for their mountain climbing trip.

      Arriving at their destination an hour and a half later Russ and Rose exited his car and walked to the ticket booth. They stood in a short line for a few minutes before buying their entry passes. Walking into the park their guide led them to the first group of climbers. Once they

Before The Flower Withers   by Dennis C Mariotis

reached the maximum number in the group the instructor spoke to them and explained what to do. About fifteen minutes later everyone was in a harness and ready to climb. It was a beginners group but it still took strength and stamina to climb up the hundred foot mountain.

When the climb began, the first twenty feet seemed to go by pretty well. Rose started feeling the effects of her exertion but kept up since there were others in the group who were very much out of shape and out of condition. Stopping and restarting was the norm with this group. At about seventy feet up Rose was really starting to tire. Russ stopped with her and the rest of the group for her to catch her breath. A few others were thankful but didn't want to admit it. With about ten more feet to go Rose felt a deep sharp pain. She didn't say anything to Russ as she slowly trekked the last few feet up to the top.

As soon as the last person in the group reached the top of

Before The Flower Withers   by Dennis C Mariotis

the mountain, they all celebrated. They gave each other high fives and handshakes. They congratulated each other as if they just climbed the highest mountain in the world. For them it was probably the equivalent of a professional climber climbing Mount Everest. Rose sat on a rock next to Russ as she needed the rest. Russ said, "You did it!" Rose smiled and replied between deep breaths, "We did it. Just like everything else we did together. Well what's next?" Russ chuckled, "In about twenty minutes we're gonna climb down." Rose snickered and wiped the sweat off her brow and exclaimed, "You mean they don't have an elevator? How are we supposed to get back down?" Russ chuckled, "We can do it the hard way and carefully walk down or we can do it the easy way and take one step off the cliff over there." Rose laughed as did some of the other climbers nearby who overheard their conversation.

Suddenly Rose's expression quickly turned from a smile into a grimace as she groaned out loud and doubled over from a deep sharp

Before The Flower Withers   by Dennis C Mariotis

pain. Russ grabbed her and asked, "What's the matter grandma?" Hearing her cry out, others as well as the guide quickly walked over to her. He asked, "What's going on here? Are you okay?" Rose turned to him and said, "I'll be okay. I'm just feeling some really bad pain in my chest." The guide replied, "Just do your best to relax ma'am. I'll radio for help and we'll get you down right away!" Turning to the others who gathered to see what was going on, the guide said to them. "This lady needs room to breathe. And I need you to get back to the designated area where we will begin to our decent down to the ground."

As the crowd moved away from her, the sound of a helicopter was heard heading their way. Rose smiled and said to Russ, "I guess I found a third and even easier way to get down!" Russ chuckled as he held her hand and said, "See? I told you! Every one of you bucket list items comes with very unusual and memorable results." They laughed when Rose replied, "Yeah well? Why do anything half-assed when you can

Before The Flower Withers   by Dennis C Mariotis

take something routine and add excitement and drama?"

        With the helicopter sitting on the landing area, the trained medical evacuation crew loaded Rose on a stretcher and into the helicopter. Sitting next to her, Russ held her hand as he rode with her until they reached the landing area on the ground below. There they were greeted by an ambulance that took her to the nearest hospital. Russ followed behind and parked his car in the hospital parking lot. Exiting his car and entering the hospital he met up with Rose in a room in the Emergency Room.

        He sat by her side and watched the monitors she was hooked up to flash and beep. Within an hour a doctor walked in to check on Rose. He told them that everything looked fine as far as her heart was concerned. Knowing about her terminal cancer after consulting with Dr. Bill before coming into her room he said that he was going to discharge her with orders to see Dr. Bill immediately. This did not require

Before The Flower Withers   by Dennis C Mariotis

an ambulance ride from Helen, Georgia to Marietta since she did not have a condition that warranted the need for emergency transport. The doctor released her to Russ with instructions. Russ drove his car to the hospital doors and waited as the nursing crew assisted Rose into his car. Driving off they arrived at Dr. Bill's office in about two hours. There he examined her and finding that it was all from the over exertion he monitored her for about an hour before releasing her to go home.

When she arrived, her daughters were there waiting inside her home. She was happy to see them and they were happy and relieved to see that she walked in without any assistance. Russ stayed for a little while but he left shortly after as his mother and his aunt tended to all Rose's needs. Before leaving Rose had him sit down next to her so they could chat regarding the last item on her bucket list. Rose said, "Come by in a couple of days so I can take care of the last thing on my list."

Before The Flower Withers   by Dennis C Mariotis

With a puzzled look Russ asked, "You mean you know what you're gonna do to change and impact someone's life?" She nodded and answered, "Yeah. I planned this about a month ago. I'm experiencing a lot of the things Dr. Bill said I would and I didn't want to tell you about them until now. I know the end is near." Russ swallowed hard and shook his head, "Can I do anything for you?" Russ let out a short chuckle and Rose snickered when she answered, "Unless you can walk on water, make the blind see, and bring the dead back to life, *there's nothing you can do!* But you can take me on a short ride for my final mission." Russ nodded asking, "Where do you want to go?" Rose answered, "I'll tell you when you get here. Now go and get some much needed rest and don't worry about me! Okay?" Russ hugged her, kissed her cheek, and sighed, "Okay. See you in a couple of days!" Then he stood up and left her house. After he left, Rose sat back and grimaced in pain and tried to hide it from her family so they wouldn't worry.

CHAPTER 15
Changing A Family's World

Rose's health took a turn for the worse almost immediately after her episode from mountain climbing landed her in the hospital. The climbing had nothing to do with her failing health, but rather from her medical condition progressively deteriorating like Dr. Bill told her it would. A couple of days later Russ arrived at Rose's house. He rang the doorbell but didn't wait for Rose to answer it. Russ had

Before The Flower Withers   by Dennis C Mariotis

the key to her house and unlocked the door. Ringing the doorbell was just a signal that someone was coming in. As he slowly opened the front door Russ called before walking in, "Hello? Grandma it's me Russ!"

Rose sat up on the couch and called to him, "Come in honey." Russ walked in, closed the door behind him, and walked over to the couch. Before sitting down he bent over and gave Rose a hug and a kiss on her cheek. Then he sat down next to her. He grinned at her and said. "I'm so glad to see you!" She chuckled and replied, "After the other day I'm so glad to see anyone!" Russ asked, "How are you feeling today?" Rose nodded and closed her eyes for a few seconds. Then she opened them and answered, "I'm getting much weaker and the pain is sometimes more than I can take but I'm managing. Your mom and aunt are helping me a lot." Russ asked, "Can you still get around all right on your own?" She snickered, "Most of the time yes. Of course I'm not gonna win any marathons

Before The Flower Withers   by Dennis C Mariotis

but I can still get a spurt of energy that lets me get here or there."

Russ nodded and asked, "Are are ready to tackle your last item or do you want to do that another day?" Rose shook her head and with a stern expression and a serious tone she answered, "I'm ready. I don't know how much time I have left and I don't want to put anything off. A day to me now is like a lifetime to a healthy person. I've already changed my clothes. Wait here while I put my shoes on."

Rose moaned as she stood up and straightened out before turning and walking to her bedroom for her shoes. Slipping on her shoes she walked back into the living room where she locked arms with Russ and walked out of the house. Russ realized that she needed much more assistance than usual so he kept a very snug hold on her and helped guide her steps out the door, down the porch steps, and into his car. He noticed how much she weakened in just a few days.

Before The Flower Withers   by Dennis C Mariotis

Backing out of her driveway he heading down the road. Stopping at the stop sign at the end of the block he asked, "Okay. So where am I taking you and what are your plans?" Rose answered, "Turn right here and take me downtown to the Saint Peter's Homeless Shelter." Surprised Russ asked, "What are we going there for? That's a pretty rough area, and the people in that shelter can get a little unruly." Rose shook her head and answered, "I know. I've been there a few times about six months ago." Surprised again Russ asked, "What for?"

Looking around the neighborhood as he drove Rose sighed and pointed out the window, "See that house at the end of the block?" Russ replied, "Yes. That's the Johnson's house. I haven't been there in awhile." Rose replied, "Neither have they!" Puzzled Russ asked, "What?" Rose looked at him, "I guess while you were away at school your parents didn't tell you." Russ replied, "No, I don't recall them telling me anything about them except that they were really good friends and

Before The Flower Withers   by Dennis C Mariotis

helped you a lot before and after grandpa. What happened to them?"

Rose shook her head and explained, "A while ago Jerry lost his job and about the same time Mary got really sick. With all the medical bills piling up and trying to raise three kids, they ran out of money. Long story short they wound up losing everything." Russ shook his head, "Oh my God. I didn't know. So is that why we're going to the shelter?" Rose snickered, "I wanna see them again one last time and show them how much they mean to me." Russ replied, "Oh I get it now. You wanna visit them and give them some money to help them get out of there and start a new life." Rose shook her head and said, "I'm not gonna give them any money! I'm gonna give them something better."

Russ was puzzled again as he didn't understand what Rose was going to do to change an entire family's life. Russ shrugged his shoulders and watching the road he asked, "I give up. What are you

Before The Flower Withers   by Dennis C Mariotis

planning to give them that would change their world besides money?" Rose smiled and said, "Think about it my handsome college boy! If you were in their position right now, what would you want more than anything else in the world?"

It didn't take but a few seconds for Russ to come up with the right answer. Tapping his head with his hand he said, "How could I **not** realize that right away? If I was in a homeless shelter, what I would want more than anything would be...*a home*, of course!" Rose nodded and said, "That's exactly right. Now I award you a PhD!" Russ asked, "But how are you gonna do that?" Rose answered, "It's all spelled out in my Will. Over the past year I slowly gave away most of my valuables to your mom and Aunt Helen. They'll also split over three hundred thousand dollars in stocks and bonds that I saved up as well as another fifty thousand in savings. And as for my house, well the Johnson's need it more than anyone I know. Jerry is a master carpenter. For all the work Jerry did for us over the years when grandpa was too sick to do

Before The Flower Withers   by Dennis C Mariotis

it, he never charged us a penny. Now it's my turn to do something good for them."

Russ smiled and looked at Rose for a second, "You know grandma, that's the best thing you could do. You are gonna change the world for an entire family. But one question: Don't the Johnson's have creditors that are gonna come after the house when they get it?" Rose answered, "That's already been taken into consideration. They declared bankruptcy a while ago so they have a clean slate and soon they'll have a home without a mortgage to live in, and reestablish their lives." Arriving at the shelter Russ exited the car and helped Rose out. Rose winked at him and said, "Now let's go give them the good news."

Arriving at Rose's house later that night Russ helped her inside. His mom was there since it was her turn to watch Rose. Later that night Rose suffered great amounts of pain. Her daughter called for an ambulance to take Rose to the hospital.

Before The Flower Withers   by Dennis C Mariotis

CHAPTER 16
The Flower Withers

Four o'clock in the morning Russ' phone rang several times before it startled him. Waking up and rubbing his eyes Russ looked to see who was calling him so early. Seeing it was his mother caused his kidneys to gush out the adrenalin that brought him out of his zombie state and into full throttle as he loudly said, *"Grandma!"* Tapping his phone as he quickly snapped up in his bed he spoke, "Mom? Is it

Before The Flower Withers   by Dennis C Mariotis

grandma?" He heard his mother's voice cracking on the other end as she answered, "Yeah! About an hour ago I called 911 because she was having so much pain and her medication wasn't helping at all." Hearing this obviously distressed Russ. Swallowing hard as he tried to be strong for his mom he asked, "Is grandma alive?"

His mom sniffled throughout the conversation as she answered, "Yes. Barely. She's in the ICU at Saint Mary's General Hospital. She's conscious and she wants to see you so I called you first. She's very very weak. The doctors told us that she could go anytime." Russ held his emotions and replied, *"I'm on my way!"*

It took about two minutes for Russ to change his clothes and run out the door and into his car. Cranking it up, he floored the gas pedal and fishtailed down the street. He made it to the hospital in less than fifteen minutes. All the way he was hoping and praying he could see her and talk to her one last time. Exiting his

Before The Flower Withers   by Dennis C Mariotis

car he ran as fast as he could into the hospital and up two flights of stairs to the ICU. Seeing his mother standing outside and looking into the room he walked up to her and hugged her, "How is she?" His mother answered after wiping her eyes and nose, "No change since I called you."

Looking into the ICU Russ saw Rose in a bed hooked up to all sorts of tubes. She had her eyes half open. Walking up to the nurses' station he asked them if he could see Rose. At the station was the attending ICU physician busy writing his notes. He looked at Russ and said, "I looked in on her a few minutes ago. I'm surprised that she was able to hold a short conversation. Are you Russ?" He answered, "Yes sir." The doctor said, "She kept asking for you. You can go in and see her provided you don't do anything to put her in any distress." Russ nodded, "Thank you doctor."

Russ slowly walked up to his mother who was now accompanied by his Aunt Helen. He told them that the

Before The Flower Withers   by Dennis C Mariotis

doctor allowed him to see her. They waited as Russ slowly walked into the room and over to Rose's bedside. He gently put his hand over hers and softly spoke to her, "Grandma. It's me Russ. Can you hear me?" Rose slowly opened her eyes the rest of the way and nodded. Since she was able to breathe on her own she didn't have any tubes to obstruct her mouth. Struggling to talk she said with a weak voice as she managed a grin, "I wanted to see you one last time and tell you how much I love you and how much fun I had."

Holding back his tears he spoke to her, "We had the best time ever. But try not to struggle." With labored breathing she smiled and said, "I couldn't have done it without you. I feel like I've done more living in the last three months than I did in the last seventy five years." Russ smiled and said, "I'm so glad I got to share every minute of that with you! So what do you want me to do now?" In between her shallow breathing she smiled and said, "Remember when you told me to take my bet off the Craps table?" Russ

Before The Flower Withers   by Dennis C Mariotis

smiled and said, "Yeah." Rose kept her smile and continuously breathing shallow she replied, "Well it's time for you to take back your bet since you put your money on me." Remembering what he said to her about putting his money on her beating out the Grim Reaper he couldn't help but smile.

"Russ?" she asked. He answered, "I'm right here grandma." With an even harder time she managed to say, "Promise me something?" He replied, "Sure. What is it?" She said, "Promise me you'll never forget me and every time you think about me you'll laugh. I don't want you to cry for me. I'll be watching you from Heaven and if I see you crying I'll feel really bad. Okay?" Russ nodded and choked back his tears, "I promise." Rose smiled and said, "Good boy. I saw your grandpa earlier and he's waiting for me. Now it's time for me to get some rest." After she said that she closed her eyes but kept her smile. Within a few seconds Russ felt her hand go limp as the ICU buzzer sounded. Rose quietly and peacefully passed away.

Before The Flower Withers   *by Dennis C Mariotis*

Russ let her hand go and stepped back to let the nurses and doctor rush in and take their place by Rose. Examining her for a minute, the doctor looked over to Russ and said, "I'm sorry young man." Russ nodded but did not shed a tear. Looking at his mother who stood by the window holding her sister and crying, Russ stepped over to Rose's bedside. He leaned down and gave her a kiss on the cheek and said, "Thanks for helping me understand the great things about living. Get your rest and tell grandpa I love him and I miss him too." Russ stood up and smiled as he looked at her laying there so peacefully with a smile on her face. Then he walked out of the room and hugged his mother and aunt and consoled them.

As more relatives finally showed up Russ excused himself and left the hospital. It was now almost eight o'clock in the morning. The sun was shining and the sky was clear. Russ drove around for awhile, then he stopped at a park that his grandmother used to take him to when he

Before The Flower Withers   by Dennis C Mariotis

was a child. He walked over to a bench where she once bounced him on her knees and sat down. More memories came to him as he sat there and listened to the sounds of nature. Then he looked up at the sky and said, "I know I promised you grandma but I'm only gonna do this once."

Taking a large tissue out of his pocket, he bent his head over, and cried. After about a minute Russ' cry was interrupted by a beautiful dove that flew by him and bulls eye! It dropped of a load of bird poop right on the top of his head. Russ looked up and realized what the bird did. Using the tissue, he wiped his eyes first. Then he looked up at the Heavens as he wiped the droppings off his head. He laughed out loud for a few seconds. Then he stopped and, as if he was talking to Rose, said, *"You learned that trick in France! I only wish it was ice cream. Okay grandma, I got your message!"*

CHAPTER 17
A Fun Tribute To Rose

Funeral services for Rose were held three days later at Jackson's Funeral Home. Family and friends gathered to pay their last respects to Rose Miles. The stage was set up with a large silver screen and a projector. In front of the stage there was a beautiful long rectangular stand. In the middle of the stand sat an

Before The Flower Withers   by Dennis C Mariotis

ornate urn containing Rose's cremated ashes. Behind the urn was an eight by ten picture of Rose. Surrounding the urn and her picture were pictures of Rose's family. When the services began it was Rose's long time family Pastor and friend, Reverend Daniel who delivered the opening prayer. When he finished he gave a short homily about life and death. Everyone sat patiently and listened. Some people wiped their eyes as they sat and listened. Others heard this so many times before that they fidgeted in their seats.

When he completed his homily he invited anyone to come forward and speak about the life and times of Rose Miles. Several people came forward and spoke. Some made the audience snicker while others such as Jerry Johnson and his family touched everyone deeply with his story of what a great sacrifice Rose made and how she changed his family's life forever. Sitting in the far back with tears in their eyes were three other lives she touched. Garth, Stoner, and Boots were dressed in their best biker outfits and

Before The Flower Withers   by Dennis C Mariotis

drove their bikes all the way from Las Vegas to attend her funeral. Across from them were some players from the Atlanta Braves along with the umpire that Rose knocked out when she threw out the baseball.

The last non-family person who came up to speak was escorted by Rose's son-in-law. Officer Joe walked up to the podium with a man who went by his first name only. In a heavy southern Georgia accent he spoke, "Hey y'all. My name is Jay and I want to tell y'all my experience with this here fine lady. A while ago I did a bad thang. Early in the mornin' I used a gun to rob a poor ol' boy in a convenience store. When the poe-leese come after me I tried to outsmart them buy jacking their car. And while I was sittin' in the front seat I heard the sound of a shotgun being loaded coming from behine' me. Then I felt the barrel pressed up agin' my head. That scared me out of my briches. To my surprise it was this poor ol' woman Rose holding that Remington on me. Well anyway I'm in jail now. But I have to say that I

Before The Flower Withers   by Dennis C Mariotis

come here today to say thank you to that ol' gal. If it wasn't for her I wouldn't have found my callin'. From now on I'm playin' it straight. I'm learning a trade that's gonna pay me plenty. When I get outta jail in five years I'm gonna be a television preacher! Thank the Lord. And thank you 'Shotgun Grandma Rose'. God bless you!" People in the audience shook their heads while others laughed under their breath.

      The last person to speak was Russ. Walking up to the podium, he carried a box with him. He greeted everyone, "Hello friends and family and honored guests. Thanks for coming to my grandma's final farewell." The audience was quiet and attentive. Russ continued, "Today I'm not saying goodbye. I'm saying until we meet again to my best friend, Grandma Rose. I had the great experience of being with her for her last three months and helping her accomplish things on her bucket list. Those were three of the best months I ever lived. I've got a slide show of these events and trust me,

Before The Flower Withers   by Dennis C Mariotis

you're not gonna wanna miss any of them. I know she enjoyed them because she told everyone about them. Before I show you the pictures I have to apologize to Reverend Daniel and anyone else who may be offended."

Pausing a moment Russ turned on the projector. He asked the ushers to turn out the lights. Then the slide show began. The audience laughed and cheered as Russ showed them the pictures he took of all her bucket list experiences. They laughed at the Frenchman with his ice cream covered head. They ooo'd and ahh'd at the sight of the Eiffel Tower and Rose petting a lion cub. They gasped at the pictures of a python around her shoulders and at Rose dangling off the edge of a building nine hundred feet off the ground. The umpire even laughed at a picture of him with two black eyes and cotton extending from both nostrils courtesy of Rose's wild pitch. The slide show went on for about twenty minutes and never once did any picture get less than a five star reaction.

Before The Flower Withers   *by Dennis C Mariotis*

When the slide show ended and the lights came back on, Russ addressed the audience. He said, "I was with Rose in her final seconds of life. She made me promise to not cry when I thought about her but to always laugh and remember the great times together. She taught me so much about love and life in a few months. I'll miss her. Before I finish I want to share a few more things with you. This is simple wisdom she shared with me." Pausing a couple of seconds Russ pulled out a few sheets of paper and read from them. He said, "Aside of the obvious rules of morality, Rose lived by very simple rules."

Reading from a sheet of paper that was given to him by Rose he said, "They are:

DANCE like no one's watching.
SING like no one's listening.
LIVE each day as if there's no tomorrow.
LAUGH until your stomach hurts
LOVE as though you never had a broken heart.
HUG me as if it's the last time you'll see me."

Before The Flower Withers   by Dennis C Mariotis

Russ put down that sheet of paper, then reading from the next one he held he continued, "Here's a poem that I wrote for my grandma Rose. The title of this poem is, *'Before The Flower Withers'*." Clearing his throat he took a deep breath and choked back his emotions. Then he read:

"Before The Flower Withers.

Smell the flowers in your life every day,
Because eventually they'll wither away!
Don't hurry by without a glance,
Always admire them with every chance.
They're only here for a season,
And they exist for a reason.
Stop and take your precious time,
And gaze upon their beautiful design.
Don't neglect them but help them grow.
See their splendor and then you'll know,
That you found complex beauty and simple truth.
All should do this from the aged to the youth.
Smell the flowers in your life every day,
Because eventually they'll wither away!"

Taking a couple of deep breaths before he continued, Russ put the paper containing his poem down. Then smiling before the final item of his speech Russ said, "Rose always tried to end everyday on a good note.

Before The Flower Withers   by Dennis C Mariotis

So the last thing I have is a limerick that I wrote for her." Russ looked up at his friends and winked when he heard them laugh for a few seconds before continuing, "She loved limericks and knew quite a few of them." Reading from a paper he recited:

"A Limerick for Rose:

Rose was once a beautiful flower,
Who confronted death and did not cower.
She rode a highway with Bikers,
Climbed a mountain with Hikers
And lived a full life in her last hour."

When he finished reading it, Russ thanked the audience, who in turn stood up and clapped as he stepped down from the stage and walking past Rose's urn, he touched it before taking his seat. Then Reverend Daniel stood up and ended the services with a closing prayer. People gathered around afterwards and spoke with Rose's family before going into the banquet room and eating the catered food. Russ showed pictures he couldn't show to the audience to his friends and other guests. There was a lot of laughter and smiles as they celebrated the life of Rose Miles.

Before The Flower Withers   by Dennis C Mariotis

CHAPTER 18
Russ Completes The List

Thirty years later finds Russ married with two grown children of his own. After coming home from a trip to Europe with his wife he unpacked his bags and set his camera on his desk. Later that night he spent several hours printing pictures and making a small collage. The next morning Russ, accompanied by his wife of twenty five years walked into his office. She smiled and hugged him when she saw what he put together.

Before The Flower Withers   by Dennis C Mariotis

Russ kept Rose's urn in his large office after his mother moved into a nursing home. He had an area set up beautifully to honor the woman who taught him so much about life. Around the urn he displayed pictures from all the events of her bucket list.

Last night he finished it by including all the things on Rose's list that she couldn't get to do. He kept his promise and fulfilled the list by bringing a picture of them together while accomplishing everything else on the list.

Along with the pictures was the original bucket list he wrote with Rose. A couple of notes taped to the urn stated; *'Sorry Grandma but no swimming with sharks!'* and *'I left our picture in the hotel safe while I was on my honeymoon! LOL!'* Next to the original list he included the list of other things he did on her behalf. This is the list he included:

Before The Flower Withers   by Dennis C Mariotis

ROSE & RUSS's BUCKET LIST.

- ✓ *Visit the Acropolis*
- ✓ *Visit the Pyramids of Egypt*
- ✓ *Visit Rome's Coliseum*
- ✓ *Skydive*
- ✓ *Ride in a Hot Air Balloon*
- ✓ *Run with the Bulls in Spain*
- ✓ *Sail on a Yacht*
- ✓ *Drive a Race Car around the Race Track*
- ✓ *Take a Cruise*
- ✓ *A Trip to Hawaii*
- ✓ *Cross Country Bicycle Ride*
- ✓ *See the Grand Canyon*

THE END

Before The Flower Withers   by Dennis C Mariotis

This is a picture of the author's sister and one of the strongest women in his life; his sister Vicky who survived several stage 4 cancers and lived 21 years beyond ALL medical expectations.

Rest In Peace Vicky,

Always and forever in my heart!

Denny

Made in the USA
Middletown, DE
14 October 2022